PUPPY WISHES & CANDY KISSES

JENNIFER FAYE

Lazy Dazy Press

Published by Lazy Dazy Press

Thanks & much appreciation to:

Editor: Lia Fairchild

CONTENTS

ABOUT THIS BOOK...

THREE HOMELESS PUPPIES, TWO **lonely hearts, and a massive snowstorm.**

Candace "Candi" Goodman, an unemployed school teacher, is always sharing a smile and helping those around her. This Christmas she has volunteered to drive three puppies to a shelter in Maine. However, when a road closure sends her on a detour, she gets lost in a snowstorm.

Michael Bishop, a township road supervisor, has spent the past two years mourning the loss of his young family. As he's plowing snow late one evening, he notices something amiss. When he goes to investigate, he finds a woman and three puppies in a dire situation. The more time they spend time together, the more he finds himself falling for her mistletoe kisses. But will it be enough for him to take a chance on love again?

The Kringle Falls, Vermont series:
Book 1 – *Puppy Wishes & Candy Kisses*
Book 2 – *Puppy Love & Snowflake Kisses*
Book 3 – *Puppy Smooches & Peppermint Kisses*
Book 4 – *Puppy Hugs & Mistletoe Kisses*

CHAPTER ONE

THE SNOWFLAKES GREW IN number.

The wipers struggled to clear the windshield.

This early December winter storm had Candace "Candi" Goodman turning up the speed of the wipers while easing up on the accelerator. She squinted into the night, trying to ascertain her position on the snow-covered roadway. It was impossible to make out the edge of the road.

Worse yet, there was nowhere to pull over. No signs of civilization anywhere. She had to keep pushing slowly onward until there was a safe place to stop for the night. Just then there was whimpering from the back of the minivan. She wondered if the puppies could sense her heightened stress level.

"It's okay, babies." She wished she believed her own words. She didn't feel like any of this was okay. "Don't worry. I won't let anything happen to you."

Maybe if she said it enough times, she'd eventually believe it. But ever since an accident had the highway completely shut down and she'd been directed onto an alternate road, she felt as though she were going in the wrong direction.

Still, she'd turned right onto North Route 3 like her phone's GPS had instructed. So, at least she was headed in the right direction. Her destination was a no-kill shelter in Maine, where these three pups could be adopted.

She regularly volunteered at Bob's Animal Friends Shelter just outside of Cleveland, Ohio. When the owner, Bob Higgins, who was getting up in age, became very ill and was hospitalized, they needed to empty the shelter for the holidays. It wasn't an easy task. After she'd placed all but these last three puppies, a shelter in Maine was willing to take them.

After a school consolidation, Candi, being one of the newest hires, had been let go. Now, working as a substitute teacher until a full-time position opened up, her schedule was flexible. It made it possible for her to make this road trip.

With Christmas carols playing, she'd set off at 5:00 a.m. Her goal was to make it to Maine in one day. It wouldn't be easy with such a long drive, but she decided it would be too hard to find lodging with not one but three excitable four-month-old puppies. With Christmas just a few weeks away, the sooner she got them to the new shelter, the sooner the puppies would find their forever homes.

The only thing she hadn't taken into account was the weather, or should she say the unexpected change in weather. It wasn't that she hadn't checked the forecast. She most certainly had, but the rain they were supposed to get had now turned into snow. Lots of snow.

It wasn't so bad on the highway, because it was being maintained. But this rural road wasn't in such good shape. Between the bad weather and the early darkness of winter, it was making it difficult to find her way back to the highway.

She squinted, hoping to see past the army of snowflakes. Where had the cars gone that she'd been following when they were redirected off the highway? They had either gotten swallowed up in the snowstorm or they'd turned off a ways back.

As the roadway narrowed, she had a feeling she'd made a wrong turn. She glanced at her phone, which was mounted on the dash. Why wasn't it saying anything? Checking her mirrors and finding herself completely alone on this road, she stopped. She picked up her phone and found that it had no signal. A frustrated groan started deep in her throat.

Her gut told her to turn around, but there was no safe place to do that. On her left was a hillside, and to her right was a steep embankment. The last thing she wanted was to end up in a ditch on this desolate road in a snowstorm. Her only choice was to keep going.

She let off the brake and proceeded along the road, all the while peering into the night for a signpost that might tell her what road she was on. She'd even appreciate knowing what town she was nearing, but so far, she hadn't found any signs.

The large snowflakes were mesmerizing in the headlights. She blinked repeatedly, trying not to get caught up in the hypnotic motion of the snow.

Even the Christmas music had stopped playing. The only sound right now was the crunch of the snow under the van's tires. She had never felt more alone.

As she climbed a grade, her tires started to spin. Her instinct was to stop, but she knew if she did, she probably wouldn't get moving again. And there was no way she wanted to get stuck out there in the middle of nowhere.

One of the puppies let out a whine. She couldn't blame him. It had been a long day—a very long one. They'd made numerous pitstops along the way for the puppies to stretch their legs, which only made this trip feel longer.

She'd hoped to be closing in on the Maine state border by now. Instead, she didn't have a clue where they were.

"It's okay." She tried to keep the worry from her voice.

The puppy whined again.

Her gaze moved to her phone. The screen was dark now. She didn't even waste the time it would take to wake it and see if there was a signal yet. Instead she focused all of her attention on keeping the van on the road.

As the puppy continued to whine, she decided a Christmas song was in order. It might help calm all of them, especially herself. The lyrics to "I'll Be Home For Christmas" crossed her lips. She didn't know all of the lyrics, but she sang the ones she knew and made up the rest. The more she sang, the quieter the puppy grew. At least someone liked her singing. If only it were that easy to fix all the world's problems.

And then out of the corner of her eye, she spotted something moving into the roadway. Her heart launched into the back of her throat. She didn't have time to think. She reacted.

Candi stomped the brake with both feet. The van didn't slow down. It continued to glide across the icy asphalt.

The breath hitched in Candi's lungs. This was bad. So very bad.

She cut the steering wheel hard to the right. Every muscle in her body stiffened. She waited for the collision.

It didn't happen.

Instead, the front wheels dropped off the edge of the roadway. The van continued to career off the road and down an embankment.

She screamed but there was no one to hear her...except the pups. They started barking and howling. They were all going to die and it was all her fault. If only she hadn't gotten lost.

She'd heard that in a person's final moments, their life flashes before their eyes. It didn't for her. All she could think about was how she'd let Bob down. And what would happen to the sweet puppies behind her.

The screech of metal against rock pierced her ears. Tree branches scraped against the windows. The puppies let out terrified cries.

Candi was bounced in her seat. The only thing holding her in place was her seatbelt.

And then the van jerked to a stop. She slammed forward. The seatbelt strained against her shoulder and chest. She bounced side to side. Her head hit hard against the driver's side window.

It had been a long day and night.

Michael sat behind the steering wheel of one of Kringle Falls's snow plows. As the township's road supervisor, he made himself available to fill in where needed. Tonight, he'd been needed as a snow system moved through the area and with the flu making the rounds, they were shorthanded. It was a bit early in the season for this large amount of snow, but it wasn't unheard of either.

He knew many people in Kringle Falls would be thrilled by the white stuff. As they said, it added to the atmosphere of living in a Christmas town—the biggest and jolliest in the country. He didn't know if it was true, but this town definitely played into the theme.

With this winter storm, he'd been behind the steering wheel for hours now. It was getting late. No one should be on these roads at this hour.

After he made this final pass up Reindeer Pass, he was calling it a night. He'd go home and get a few hours of sleep before he hit the roads again. The storm was supposed to end sometime in the morning. The forecasters had predicted at sunup, but after having a job that was weather-related, he knew for a fact that the forecast was wrong more than it was right.

He reached for a tall thermal mug and took a sip of the still-warm coffee. It'd tasted better a couple hours ago.

As he slid the cup back into its holder, he pulled to a stop at an intersection. It was there he noticed a set of tire tracks that were headed up the ridge. *Why would anyone go up there in this weather?*

There were no houses along that stretch of roadway. It must be some kids testing themselves and their vehicle out on these treacherous roads. It gave him an uneasy feeling in the pit of his stomach. If they got stuck out there, it would be hours, no, more like days, until anyone found them.

So much for rushing home to bed. He turned toward the ridge and followed the tracks. He was pretty certain he'd find some teenage kids stuck in the snow.

The fact he could still make out the tire tracks was a good sign. It meant if they did get stuck, they wouldn't have been out in the frigid temperatures for long.

Thoughts of his warm, cozy bed were long forgotten as he continued up the ridge. There was a lot of drifted snow in these parts. Just then a gust of wind sent the snow flying, and momentarily there was a whiteout. He hated nights like this because there was always someone who thought they could best Mother Nature. In the end, Mother Nature always won.

When the wind calmed, he could still make out the now faint indentation of tire tracks. As long as they made it to Blitzen Crossing, they should be okay.

But when he crested Donner Ridge, the tracks stopped. He stepped on the brakes. Where had they gone?

He looked all around, but there was no sign of the vehicle responsible for making those tracks. He muttered under his breath as he quickly shrugged on his heavy coat and yanked on an orange knit hat.

Grabbing a flashlight, he got out. As soon as his foot touched the ground, his boot slid. Luckily, he was still holding on to the door. It was the only thing that kept him upright. The road was now nothing more than a sheet of ice.

Once he regained his balance, he carefully moved to the edge of the road. He backtracked, searching for the tire tracks. His gut told him that someone was in trouble.

He swung the beam of the light back and forth across the roadway. He was about ten feet behind the snowplow when he found the end of the tire tracks.

They swerved to the side of the roadway and then disappeared down over the embankment. He followed the tracks with the flashlight, but the foliage was so dense he wasn't able to see the vehicle.

He reached for his phone and dialed 9-1-1, but the call didn't go through. When he looked at the screen, he saw there was no signal. He knew cell signals were spotty at best this far from town, but he was hoping in this instance he would get lucky. He walked in a big circle, waving the phone around, trying to locate a signal. He didn't have any luck.

He glanced back at his truck. All of the lights were on, including the flashing yellow light atop the cab. If anyone ventured out on this desolate road, they'd definitely be able to see his parked truck.

He turned to the embankment. Not sure what he'd encounter, he started down the steep slope. It wasn't easy with the snow hiding the rocky terrain.

Between the darkness, the uneven terrain, and the heavy vegetation, it was hard to keep his balance. At one point, his foot slipped and he fell on his backside. He struggled to regain his footing. Not bothering to brush off the snow, he kept going. Every moment that went by could be critical.

"Hello!" he called out, hoping someone would respond to him.

Silence was the only response.

He continued to follow the broken tree limbs and the trampled bushes. It couldn't be much farther.

And then the beam from his flashlight caught on something reflective. As he drew closer, he realized it was the backend of a vehicle.

His steps quickened. "Hey! Can you hear me?"

There was still no response.

He mentally braced himself as he neared the vehicle. He had no idea what he was going to find when he glanced inside the van. But then he heard something. It was faint, but it was there. But what was it?

CHAPTER TWO

I T HAD ALL HAPPENED so fast.

One moment they were on the road, and the next they were here.

Candi sat back in her seat and glanced around. It was so dark it was hard to make out anything but the branches pressing against the windows.

All three of her precious cargo were panic-barking. They were alive. That was the important part. But she worried that they might be injured.

As she worked to release her seatbelt, she realized that during the accident, the engine had died. The cold of the evening was quickly seeping into the van.

She tried to restart the engine. Nothing happened. *No-no-no. It has to start.* They needed the heat because the last time she'd looked at the outdoor temperature, it was below freezing and continuing to drop.

She tried to start the engine again and again. Then, realizing the vehicle was still in gear, she moved the gearshift to Park. She gave the ignition a few more tries. Still nothing.

The puppies were barking frantically. She needed to go check on them. Then she'd figure out what to do to get them out of this mess.

She moved to the back of the van. She was relieved to find the three musketeers, as she'd nicknamed them, moving about their crates, not showing any sign of injury. She took her first easy breath. She'd never have forgiven herself if anything had happened to them.

When she knelt before them, the pups stuck their paws through the openings in their crates as they tried to reach her. She could see the fear in their eyes.

One by one, she released the doors on their crates. They rushed out and crawled all over her. As she petted them, she studied them to make sure they were all right.

Once she'd assured herself that they hadn't been injured, her thoughts turned to finding a way to get them out of there. Because without heat, they couldn't stay there.

And then a thought came to her. She could try her phone. Her gaze moved to the holder on the dash. Her phone was no longer there. She glanced around, but it was so dark without the lights from the dashboard. It was going to be hard to find her phone.

As the puppies climbed all over her, she thought about how to get them all out of there. The only option was for her to walk for help. But how far? And what about the puppies? She couldn't just leave them in this frigid cold without heat.

---*elle*---

There was a sound.

Was it whimpering?

Michael reached the rear corner panel of the van. There were no lights on inside, and the motor wasn't running. It didn't look good.

But there was that sound again. Was it someone in pain? *Perhaps.*

He tromped through the thick snow to the driver's side door. Bracing himself for the worst, he glanced in the window. There was no one there. How could that be?

He raised his flashlight and shined it inside. Both seats were vacant. "Hello. Is anyone in there?"

"Back here!" The muffled female voice came from the back of the van.

He tried the driver's door. It wouldn't budge. "The door is locked."

He heard some shuffling and barking. *Barking?* He waited, but the door was still locked. What was taking so long? Maybe the woman was injured.

"I can break the window," he shouted.

"No! Don't. I'm coming."

There was more barking. Was it one dog? Or two? He tried to shine the flashlight into the back of the van, but he couldn't see around the seat.

And then a young woman appeared between the seats. In the light's beam, he could make out her strawberry-blond hair. It was long and pulled back in a ponytail that hung over her shoulder.

When she leaned toward the door to unlock it, he noticed a bit of blood smeared in her hair. He had no idea how seriously she might be injured. He pulled his phone from his pocket and waved it around, trying to get a signal. Still nothing. No way to get help.

When he heard the lock release, he opened the door. "You're hurt."

"I am?"

How could she not know? She must be in shock. "It's your forehead. There's some blood. You need to sit down."

"I can't. I have to get things ready to go."

"What things?" It was then he heard a chorus of barking.

"I have to grab supplies for the pups. Can I borrow your flashlight? It'll make this so much easier."

Normally, he'd insist on getting her medical attention and then coming back for the dogs, but with the falling temperature, they couldn't be left out there. However, he still wasn't sure how to get her and the dogs up the snow-covered incline. He'd figure something out.

The more she moved, the more the van rocked. Michael took the moment to step to the front of the van and was shocked when he found the van's undercarriage hung up on a tree stump. That was it. That was all that had stopped the vehicle from careening the rest of the way down the embankment.

In a perfect world, the van should be secured with lines tied to nearby trees. But he didn't have any rope or chains. And there didn't appear to be any trees nearby that were sturdy enough to hold the van in place. All he could hope was that he was able to help the woman and dogs get out of the vehicle without it breaking free of the tree trunk.

He stepped back to the open doorway. "We have to go."

"I just need a few more minutes to fill a couple more bags with supplies."

"Leave it. We'll get whatever you need in town."

"It won't take me that long to round up the things. Everything got shifted in the accident."

"I don't think you understand. This van is not secure. The more you move around, the better the chance it'll start rolling again."

"Oh."

At last, he seemed to have gotten through to her. The next thing he knew, there was a fuzzy black and white dog thrust at him.

"Take Tank." Her voice had a hard edge to it that said not to argue with her as she placed the dog on the driver's seat. "I'll take Odie and Tater Tot."

He heard the van creak. "Move slowly. I don't know how much longer the stump is going to hold it in place."

It was a big puppy—maybe a few months old. Tank sniffed him. Michael held his hand out for him to sniff. When the dog seemed okay with him, Michael gently ran his hand over the pup's back. He could feel the puppy shiver. He didn't think it was from the cold. At least not yet. It was probably from the shock of the accident.

He soon realized the dog had on a harness and a red leash. Michael took a moment to secure the leash around his hand. Then he glanced toward the back of the van. What was taking the woman so long?

Before he could vocalize the question, there was another puppy thrust at him. "Can you hold on to Odie while I put a harness on Tater Tot?"

Michael looked down at the two puppies now on the driver's seat. Odie looked to be a small cavapoo mix of some sort. They stared at him and proceeded to bark in unison. He frowned at them. Didn't they know he was there to help them?

A moment later, the woman placed a third dog on the seat. He didn't know how they all fit. He worried one of them was going to fall out into the snow. He stepped closer to use his body as a wall.

"We're ready to go," the woman said.

At last, they could get out of there. "Move carefully when you climb into the front seat. Remember, you don't want to rock the van loose."

"I know. You don't have to keep telling me."

He wanted to say it was only a reminder, but he bit back the words. Now certainly wasn't the right time for an argument.

"Can you move the pups?" she asked.

He glanced down at the three pups, who were smashed together on the driver's seat. What was he supposed to do with all three of them?

And then he got an idea. He wasn't sure it would work, but it was worth a try.

He zipped up his coat, and then he stuffed the front hem into the top of his jeans. The belt helped hold everything in position.

Then he picked up the black and white pup. He stuffed him into his jacket. It was a tight fit, but it would work until they made it to his truck.

Then he scooped up the other two pups, one under each arm. With the pups secure, he took a step back from the vehicle.

"Be careful." He had no idea about the extent of her injuries.

"Did anyone ever accuse you of worrying like a mother hen?" she asked.

His mouth gaped. No. No one had ever accused him of that. One of the pups took that moment to stick his nose into his mouth. Michael jerked his head back, sputtered, and then closed his mouth.

He opened it again to say, "Just be careful. You don't know how badly you're hurt."

He noticed that this time she didn't have a pithy comeback. When she was at last standing next to him, he noticed she was several inches shorter than him. And he had this instinctive need to protect her, but that was hard to do when he had puppies all over him.

"Let me get the puppies up to my truck, and I'll come back to help you up the hill."

"I can take one of the pups." She held out her right hand for one of them.

Michael shook his head. "I've got them." Just then the one in his jacket started squirming around. Michael moved his hand to help secure the pup's backside to keep him from working his jacket loose and falling out.

"Then let's go." She closed the van door.

It appeared she wasn't going to listen to his suggestion for her to wait. *Stubborn woman.* Oh, well, who was he to argue with her? It's not like he even knew her. And he was certain he'd never see her again after this evening.

And so, he carefully turned. It was so dark. He squinted, searching for his previous tracks in the snow. At last, he found them. However, as the incline got steeper, he had a hard time balancing himself while holding on to the pups that refused to sit still.

At one point, he lost his balance. He thought for sure they were going to tumble down the embankment. Luckily, he regained his balance just in time to save them from becoming one giant rolling snowball.

When he reached the roadway, he turned to see the woman at the bottom, struggling to get up the incline.

"I'll be right back," he said.

He didn't wait for her response. He rushed over to the snowplow. It took some quick maneuvering to step up and open the door without losing his grip on the puppies.

When at last all three puppies were in the warm cab, he made sure the emergency brake was on.

Then he secured their leashes to the steering wheel for the lack of a better option.

"Just sit down and enjoy the warmth." He turned up the fan on the heater. "I'll be right back."

They barked. He imagined they were telling him not to leave them, which was totally ridiculous because they had absolutely no idea what he'd just said.

As he carefully closed the door, he told himself to get a grip. It had been a long day and now a long evening. He just needed some sleep, and he'd be fine when the early shift rolled around.

When he made it back to the embankment, he found the woman halfway up. He rushed down to her side.

"Let me help you." He had a feeling she might bristle at the offer.

Instead, she surprised him when she nodded her head.

"Do you mind if I put my arm around your waist?" he asked.

She shook her head.

With his arm around her slender waist, he helped her the rest of the way up the embankment. She was quite light but not exactly sturdy on her feet.

When they reached the roadway, she glanced around. Her gaze came to rest on the big yellow truck. "Is that yours?"

He nodded. "Well, not technically. It belongs to the township."

"So, you're a snow plow driver?"

He didn't feel the need to correct her. So, he merely nodded. It was close enough. "My name's Michael Bishop."

She held her hand out to him. "I'm Candace Goodman, but my friends call me Candi."

His gaze moved between the smile on her face and her extended hand. At last, he took her hand in his, and immediately, he knew it was a mistake. His fingers tingled where they touched the smooth skin of her hand. The sensation pulsed up his arm and settled in his chest, giving him a funny feeling.

He pulled his hand back. "Now, let's get out of here."

"But what about my van?" She turned to stare into the darkness that had eaten any sign of her vehicle.

"There's no way it's coming out of there tonight. It might be two or three days until you can get someone out here to tow it up for you."

"Two or three days?" There was a note of agony in her voice. "That won't work."

"This is a winter storm. Things are going to take time. Come on." He moved to the truck and opened the passenger door for her. All three puppies rushed over to that side of the truck and let out a chorus of barks.

She followed him. "You don't understand."

In the light of the truck, he saw the cut on the side of her forehead was still bleeding. He leaned into the truck and opened the glove box. He pulled out some napkins. He held them out to her. When her brows drew together as confusion shone in her eyes, he pointed to her forehead. She took the napkins and pressed them to the cut.

"Let's get out of the cold." He gestured for her to get into the truck.

"I can't. If I'd have known we couldn't tow the van, I would have grabbed those supplies for the three musketeers."

For the first time that evening, he smiled. The truth was he rarely smiled at all these days. After losing his family a couple of years ago, he didn't find many things to smile about.

The woman frowned at him. "What are you so amused about?"

"Your name for the puppies." He held out a hand to assist her into the truck. "You're letting out all of the warm air."

He detected a slight huff coming from her as she ignored his hand and instead grabbed the armrest and swung herself up and into the truck.

With the woman and puppies secure in the truck, he closed the door and made his way around to the other side. Now to make it back to town and drop them off at the hospital. Then he was headed home to bed.

He opened his door and climbed inside. He was relieved to see the puppies climbing all over the woman. Michael settled into his seat, and that was when he noticed a warm sensation on the back of his right thigh and his butt. "What in the world?"

It took him a moment to figure out what had happened. And then he expelled a frustrated sigh.

"What's wrong?"

He reached for some napkins he had in the center console from his dinner. "I think one of your puppies peed on my seat."

"Oh." The corners of her rosy lips quivered, as though she were fighting to hold back a laugh.

"This isn't funny."

"No. Of course not." This time the amusement shone in her green eyes. "I'm sorry. They're housebroken, but the accident has shaken them up."

What was he supposed to say to that? No words came to mind. So, instead, he turned off the interior lights and put the truck into gear.

The only problem was that since he'd stopped to help her, a lot of snow had fallen. They were calling for more than a foot of fresh snow overnight.

He checked his gauges. He was out of salt. He'd run out a few miles back. That was why he'd been turning around and heading back to the utility shed when he'd noticed the tire tracks.

He adjusted the plow and they set off. The two smaller puppies settled on the woman's lap and barked. A lot.

The third puppy... *What was his name? Truck? No. Tank? Yes.* Tank worked his way across the seat to Michael's side. He sat there next to him, as though he were some sort of co-pilot. At least he wasn't barking.

"Do you mind if I turn on the radio?" the woman asked.

He didn't usually have it on unless there was a football game. He was used to the rumble of the road.

When he didn't immediately answer, she said, "Sometimes the music will soothe them."

He sighed. Anything was better than listening to them bark. "Go ahead."

When she had problems reaching the radio because of the dogs sitting on her, he leaned over and turned it on. It got the dogs' attention, and they momentarily quieted.

"Anything special?" he asked.

"How about some Christmas music? 'Tis the season."

He thought of telling her that Christmas music wasn't anything special around Kringle Falls, but he had a feeling she would learn all of that soon enough.

He turned on the first station with Christmas music. They were playing "Silent Night." It wasn't one of his favorite carols. But then Candace started to sing. It was soft but loud enough for him to realize she had a beautiful voice. And suddenly "Silent Night" was becoming one of his favorite carols.

The next thing he knew, the two smaller pups settled on Candace's lap. Even the dog next to him stretched out the length of his thigh. He didn't let himself get caught up in how cute they looked. He wasn't a dog person. He wasn't a cat person either. He was better off alone.

"He likes you." The woman spoke over the rumble of the plow clearing the roadway.

Michael chose to pretend as if he hadn't heard her. And yet he caught himself glancing down at the puppy, who had his eyes closed. Michael told himself that he'd only done it to make sure the pup was okay. It had absolutely nothing to do with the fuzzy white tummy that looked perfect for a pet. Because again, he wasn't a dog person.

A few miles down the road, he noticed the woman had grown quiet. When he glanced in her direction, he found her head tilted back and her eyes closed. He was no doctor, but even he knew it wasn't good to fall asleep with a head injury.

"Hey, wake up." His gaze kept shifting between her and the roadway. He leaned over and nudged her arm. "Candace, wake up."

She sat up straight and blinked her eyes. "Did I doze off?"

"You did. And you can't do that—not until you see a doctor."

"I'm fine."

"Are you a doctor?"

"No. But I feel fine."

"You realize that I don't believe you, right?"

"Whatever." She muttered something else under her breath, but he couldn't quite make it out.

She was certainly feisty. She intrigued him. He wanted to know how she ended up adopting three puppies at once. Most people were happy with one, possibly two. But this woman had the three musketeers.

It wasn't even like they were from the same litter. They were all different breeds. There must be some sort of story behind her actions. He reminded himself there wouldn't be time to hear that story. Once she was safely at the hospital, he would be on his way home. And he didn't expect for their paths to cross again.

CHAPTER THREE

S HE DIDN'T KNOW WHAT to make of him.

Candi chanced a glance at Michael. He'd yanked off the orange knit cap, and now his short dark hair was scattered as though someone had just run their fingers through the thick strands. He was definitely good-looking. Her gaze strayed to his hands. She wasn't able to see if he wore a wedding band. And then, realizing she was checking out a total stranger, she glanced away.

Still, she was so curious about this man. How could she not be? He'd appeared out of nowhere, exactly when she needed a helping hand. And yet, she couldn't quite figure him out. One moment, he was solemn and distant. The next moment, he was doing something kind for her or the pups.

His attention appeared to be laser-focused on the road. Who better to find them in this winter storm than a snow plow driver? Hopefully, he'd be able to get them to civilization.

In truth, her head was really starting to hurt, and it wouldn't stop bleeding. But she wasn't sure if the pain was due to the accident or her worry about the van. It just had to be all right. She couldn't bear to tell Bob that she'd let him down and totaled his van in the process.

It had been so dark when she got out of the van that she hadn't been able to see how much damage had been done. She'd have to wait until morning when it was towed up that steep hill.

As she watched the snow swirl, her hand ran down over Tater Tot's soft fur. The other good thing about riding in a snow plow was the fact that the rumble and vibration of the big truck had lulled the puppies to sleep.

She glanced over at Tank. She was shocked to see the pup snuggled up to this stranger. Tank never took to new people. He was usually standoffish and protective of the other puppies. It made her wonder what he knew about this man that she didn't.

Catching herself once more staring at Michael, she turned away. The last thing she wanted was to make this moment even more awkward. She looked out the window to see a lighted sign that read *Kringle Falls Hospital*.

She wanted to tell him that she didn't need to go to the hospital. But when she lowered her hand with the napkin Michael had given her, it was completely stained with blood. So, she might need a stitch or two.

He pulled up to the emergency room entrance and stopped. A handful of people turned their heads in their direction. They continued to stare at them in curiosity.

Candi could feel her cheeks growing warm. She'd never been comfortable being the center of attention, not even when she was a child performing in the school play. "I'm going to guess you don't drive your snow plow here very often."

"Why?"

"Because everyone is looking at us."

He sighed. "It's the light on top. It's very bright. Don't worry. I won't be here long."

He got out of the truck. Tank tried to follow him. When the door was shut in the pup's face, Tank barked and whimpered as he clawed at the door. Even when she called to him, the dog wouldn't listen—at least not until she raised her voice, which was not something she did very often.

Once Tank quieted down, she watched as Michael walked through the double doors and disappeared from sight. *What is he doing?*

She didn't have to wonder for long. The next thing she knew, a hospital attendant was rolling a wheelchair out through the same double doors, and he looked to be heading straight toward her. And then she spotted Michael behind the orderly. The heat in her cheeks intensified. She wasn't an invalid.

With long strides, Michael passed the man in green scrubs and opened her door. The puppies started to bark. She ignored them.

Her gaze met Michael's brown gaze. Her heart skipped a beat as heat continued to flood into her cheeks. She averted her gaze. "A wheelchair wasn't necessary."

"It wasn't my idea."

"Oh." More heat rushed to her face.

She put the puppies on the seat next to her as Michael helped her out. Once she was seated in the wheelchair, Michael grabbed two of the puppies.

"Do you want to hold them all?" Michael asked.

She didn't have a chance to answer before the attendant said, "No dogs are allowed."

Michael frowned. "I don't think you understand. These are her dogs."

"No dogs allowed." The orderly turned and pushed the wheelchair with her in it back into the hospital.

Now she was worried. "But my dogs—"

"Will be fine," the attendant said in a confident tone. "Your boyfriend can take care of them."

Her boyfriend? Nervous laughter rushed up the back of her throat. It was all she could do to smother it.

She didn't feel confident at all about this plan. Michael may have helped her, but he was still a stranger, and he didn't appear to be crazy about dogs. If they took her blood pressure now, she knew she would be in trouble.

Still, coming to the hospital had been Michael's idea. And surely she wouldn't be there long. He'd stay and wait with the pups. Right?

───── *ele* ─────

What was taking so long?

Candi felt as though she'd been in the emergency room for days when in actuality, it had only been little more than an hour.

They had checked her out from head to toe. She was told how lucky she was to have come through the accident with only a cut on her head that, thankfully, didn't need stitches. She didn't like needles. Not in the least.

They'd cleaned out the wound and applied a couple butterfly bandages. While she waited for her release papers, it was time to call Bob and confess to the accident. But then she caught sight of a big clock on the wall. It was after midnight. How had that much time passed?

There was no way she was calling him at this hour. Tomorrow morning would do to deliver the bad news. She also needed to call the shelter in Maine to let them know she'd be delayed.

The nurse appeared and went over all of the discharge instructions. Instead of having her put back on her wet clothes, which had blood smeared all over them, they gave her a set of scrubs. The attire wasn't exactly warm for such a wintery night, but at least they were clean and dry.

The only problem was that she didn't have anywhere to go. She didn't know where Michael had taken the puppies. She didn't even know how to contact Michael. She could only hope he was waiting in the parking lot for her.

She rushed to the waiting area. As soon as she walked through the doorway, she spotted him. Michael was speaking to some of the hospital staff. He was nodding his head at something one of the men said.

When he caught sight of her, Michael continued to stare at her as he said something to the man. Michael smiled and nodded. She noticed when he smiled how it eased the stress lines on his handsome face. The breath caught in her throat. He was really handsome.

As he approached her, a smile pulled at the corners of her lips. Everything was going to be all right. She breathed easier.

She walked up to him. "Hey..." She stopped herself before she said, "Hey, handsome." What was up with her? It must be the accident and the bump on the head. It had her all out of sorts.

He gave her a quick once-over. "Are you all right?"

Was that concern in his voice? It touched her. A little smile pulled at the corners of her lips. It had been a long time since she had someone care about her.

She nodded. "I'm good."

He glanced down at her hospital clothes. "Are you sure?"

"Oh, you mean the scrubs. They gave them to me because my clothes are wet from the snow and they're blood-stained."

He nodded in understanding. "And your head. Is it okay?"

She reached up to her hairline where she now sported a couple little bandages. "No stitches necessary, just these bandages."

It was only then that she noticed the dogs weren't with him. She really wasn't clicking on all cylinders. The poor pups. They must be so tired of being cooped up in the truck all of this time. She felt guilty for putting them through so much trauma that night. If only she hadn't gotten lost with that detour, they'd be in Maine by now.

She should send a text message to her contact at the shelter in Maine. She reached into her crossbody purse, but her phone wasn't there. In that moment, she recalled that her phone had fallen from the dash during the accident and got lost in the van.

She turned to Michael. "I need to go back to the van."

His brows scrunched together, as though he was wondering why in the world she would want to do that. "Not tonight. You need to rest."

"But I can't. My phone is in it. There are people I need to call."

He reached into his pocket and pulled out his phone. He held it out to her. "Here. Use mine."

"Thanks." It was a kind gesture, but she didn't reach out to take it. "But I don't know the phone numbers."

"Oh." He put the phone back into his pocket. "Your husband must be worried about you."

"There's no husband and no boyfriend." She didn't add that, until recently, there had been a boyfriend. One she'd been dating for four years, but any time the mention of marriage came up, he found every reason why "now" wasn't the time to take the next step. She finally got tired of wasting the best years of her life on someone who didn't love her enough to see a future together—even if it meant spending Christmas alone.

Michael didn't say anything else as they walked to the exit. She wondered if he was as tired as she was. It had been a really long day. A yawn escaped her lips.

"The truck is just over here." He gestured to the left.

She followed him. She couldn't wait to go to sleep. It was only then that she realized she had nowhere to stay. What was she going to do? And with three puppies, it wouldn't be easy to find a motel that would let them all stay.

She was so deep in thought that she didn't realize Michael had come to a stop, and she ran right into him. He didn't budge. He was like a giant mountain of muscle.

She jumped back. "I'm sorry. I guess I'm more tired than I thought I was."

"It's been a really long day." He opened the door to an old red pickup.

"This truck is yours?" She hadn't expected him to be driving an antique, especially in this weather.

"Don't sound so surprised. It was my grandfather's. It's a 1950 Chevy. And the engine purrs like a kitten." He looked rather pleased with himself.

"Your grandfather must have liked you."

"That and I was the only grandson who can work on engines."

Still, she was confused. "But where's the snowplow and the puppies?"

"The plow is back at the garage, and the puppies are at my place."

"Oh." She hadn't expected him to take them home.

"You surely didn't think I'd let them sit out here in a cold truck, did you?"

"Of course not." It seemed like the right answer, but she'd noticed how he'd been distant with the puppies. Usually when people saw the dogs, they would fuss over them. But not this guy. It made her curious to know more about him. Maybe it was just that it was a long day for the both of them, and he was tired. She knew that she was ready to drop from exhaustion, but she had to keep going. But where?

CHAPTER FOUR

H E WANTED HER TO go with him?

To his place?

Candi hesitated. She looked at Michael. She wasn't quite sure what she was looking for. He had friendly eyes, even if they were a bit bloodshot. And she noticed the shadows beneath his eyes. It appeared as if he hadn't gotten much sleep lately. She wondered what kept him up at night.

She'd also noticed that he said hello to a lot of people at the hospital. If he was some sort of scary person, she doubted so many people would say hello to him. And there was the fact that he'd rescued her and the puppies. If he was going to do something bad to her, he would have done it already, before he was seen in public with her.

As he held the passenger side door open for her, he frowned. "I'm not going to hurt you."

"You do realize that probably every ax murderer has said that to some victim at some point."

"Ouch!"

"What?" She looked to see where he was hurt.

He pressed a hand to his chest. "I'm wounded. I've never been compared to an ax murderer before."

"That wasn't what I meant." She felt flustered because she truly hadn't meant to insult him. "I... I was just saying that I don't know you."

"Would it help if you spoke to my mother?" He reached for his phone.

"You can't call her."

His brows scrunched together. "Why not?"

"Because it's after midnight."

"True. What about my brother? He's the sheriff of Kringle Falls. Will he do for a character witness?"

"Are you serious?" She searched his eyes. "You'd really call him if I wanted you to?"

"Most certainly."

"I feel like the next thing you're going to tell me is that your father is the mayor?"

"No. Pops would never be a politician."

"Michael Bishop, you are a very interesting man." With all of that in mind, she got into the passenger's seat.

He closed her door and walked around to the driver's side. He yawned as he started the engine. He'd probably be at home resting if it weren't for her.

"I'm really sorry about all of this," she said. "I'm sure you never expected to help a stranger with three puppies."

"I've got to admit that I didn't."

"And I feel bad that your wife is taking care of the pups."

There was a pause before he said, "There's no wife."

She noticed how his voice caught on the word *wife. Interesting.* "A girlfriend?"

"Don't have one of those either."

It was intriguing that a man his age and so handsome was unattached. Just as quickly she assured herself that none of it mattered, because she wasn't going to be around long enough for it to matter.

He sent her a sideways glance. "Are you always so talkative?"

"I just thought we should get to know each other."

"There's not much to know." As soon as he said those words, she knew there was lots to know about him. He continued. "I was born and bred in Kringle Falls. My whole family lives here. Anything else you'd like to know?"

Lots. The more she heard about him. The more she wanted to know. But as he yawned again, she realized he was exhausted. Her curiosity would have to wait for another time.

"No." But uncomfortable with the silence, she kept nervously talking. "The poor puppies. They must be wondering what happened to me." She felt as though she were failing left and right. And all she wanted to do was help Bob so he could rest and get better.

"I wouldn't worry. They seemed fine after I fed them."

Did she hear him correctly? Or was it just some wishful thinking? "You fed them?"

Michael nodded. "I used some of the food in your bags. I hope that was all right."

"Oh, yes. Thank you." He might be a bit brusque and impatient, but he appeared to have a good heart. "When I set out this morning, I had everything planned out. By now I planned to be in Portland, Maine."

"Portland? Kringle Falls isn't anywhere close to it."

She sighed. "I had a feeling you were going to say that."

"How did you end up so far off track?"

"A detour off the highway. Then my cell phone service dropped, so I didn't have the aid of GPS. Add in this snowstorm, and I got all turned around."

"It's almost like fate directed you here."

She shook her head. "I doubt it. I don't even know where here is. I've never heard of Kringle Falls."

He slowed as he approached the center of town. When he'd taken her to the hospital, she'd been distracted by the trauma of the accident. She hadn't paid much attention to the passing scenery. This time around, she planned to take it all in.

As she stared out the window, she noticed the town was all lit up. There was a big red banner over Main Street that read: *Welcome to Kringle Falls. Largest Christmas town in the world.*

"What makes this a Christmas town?" she asked as she peered out the window at all of the decorations lining the street.

He sighed. "Some of the residents go overboard with this Christmas stuff. They now have decorations up year-round."

She'd never visited a Christmas town. She was definitely intrigued. Too bad she wouldn't have time to check it out. Maybe she'd come back another time. "It sounds like a fun place to live."

"I wouldn't know." His voice held a note of irritation. "I don't participate in all of their activities. It seems like every week they come up with another idea."

"How big is the town?"

"Last I heard there were approximately fifteen hundred permanent residents."

"So, a small town."

He pulled the pickup to a stop at a red light. "With one light in the whole town. And somehow I always seem to hit it when it's red. There isn't even another vehicle in sight, and yet here we sit."

She chose to ignore his frustrated tone. "Do you live here in town?"

He shook his head as the light changed to green, and he pressed on the accelerator. "No. I live just north of town. I'd go nuts if I lived in the borough because they now have rules that everyone has to decorate their houses. It's the town's version of an HOA."

"What happens if they don't decorate their house?"

"I've heard they have a decorating committee that shows up and does it for them. And they get fined."

"Wow! They really do take Christmas seriously around here."

"Like I said, I'm glad I live outside of the town limits."

"So, you don't decorate?"

"Not one single strand of twinkle lights anywhere on my property."

"But you have to admit that putting up Christmas decorations is fun."

He chanced a glance at her with a frown on his face. His voice dropped an octave. "Don't tell me you're one of them."

"One of who?"

"Those people who go around wearing Santa hats and caroling."

She let out a laugh at the disgusted look on his face. "No. But it doesn't sound so bad to me."

Just then the pickup pulled to a stop. It was only then that she caught herself staring at him. When she turned her head, she realized they'd arrived at their destination. When he said he lived outside of the borough, he meant right beside it.

It was a little hard to make out the house in the dark. With the aid of the porch light, she discerned it was a log home. It looked to be a large two-story home.

When he turned off the ignition, she asked, "Do you live here alone?"

"I do." He got out.

She opened the door. Her feet landed on compressed snow. When she walked, it crunched under her feet.

She couldn't wait to see the puppies again. They'd really grown on her since she'd been caring for them while Bob was in the hospital. It was going to be hard giving them up, but it was for the best. Besides, her apartment building strictly forbade having pets. She was just lucky she wasn't caught having them in her place for the past five days before they set off on their road trip.

He led her up the shoveled walk just as the snow started to fall again. She didn't want to think about how much more snow was forecast.

When Michael unlocked the front door and pushed it open, she braced herself to scoop up the puppies. And yet none of them ran out. In fact, as she stepped inside, she didn't see the puppies anywhere. Nor did she hear them.

She turned to Michael. "Where are the pups?"

"I thought it would be best to corral them."

She wasn't sure what that entailed, but she knew when those three canines got together that trouble wasn't far behind. They didn't come from the same litter, but that didn't stop them from acting like brothers, and Tank was the ringleader.

He led her into the living room. She was impressed with how neat and orderly the house was. The only thing the place was missing were the personal touches—the things that make a house a home.

To the right of the living room was a closed door. "They're in here."

She didn't hear them barking. Maybe the trauma of the accident had worn them out and they were sleeping. Because as much energy as they had, they did eventually run out.

Michael opened the door. "What in the world..."

She angled her head to peek around him. There was white fluff all over the floor. She followed him into the room. The three puppies were on the double bed. They opened their eyes and lifted their heads, but that was it. It was rare to see them this tired.

Michael stepped over to the bed and picked up a piece of cloth. "This used to be a pillow." He frowned at the puppies. "Bad puppies. Bad, bad puppies."

"Stop." She moved to stand between him and the dogs. "They aren't bad. They're puppies. They don't know any better. To them everything is a play toy."

He frowned at her. Now that she had that straightened out, she turned to the pups, and they rushed to her, their tails swishing back and forth.

As she petted each of them, she gently admonished them. "You can't make a mess. You ruined the pillow." And then she realized the problem; they didn't have any of their toys. They were back in the van along with her phone.

This mess was also her fault. Tears stung the backs of her eyes, but she refused to fall apart in front of Michael. He already had a poor opinion of her. She didn't want to make it worse.

She knelt down and started to clean up the mess. She felt awful about this. All the while, she could feel Michael's gaze on her back. What was he thinking? He was probably anxious to throw them out. Not that she could blame him. They certainly hadn't been the best of guests.

When she glanced over her shoulder to apologize for the mess, he was gone. She wondered where he'd gone, but she didn't have time to ponder it, because she had three needy puppies to look after and pillow stuffing that was scattered all over the room. If she didn't know better, she'd think the three musketeers had been throwing the fluff at each other.

"You can put the stuff in here." There was a grumbly tone to Michael's voice.

When she turned, he was holding a garbage bag out to her. Her gaze met his. "Thank you. Maybe I should take them outside first so they don't have any accidents."

"I cleaned a spot for them just outside the kitchen door. If you want, I can take them out for you."

"You would do that?" Her surprise had her uttering her thoughts without screening them. "I meant to say thank you. It is very thoughtful of you."

He reached for the leashes on the dresser. Then he knelt down. "Come."

To her utter amazement, all three of the pups ran over to him. They never did that for her. She told herself it was his deep, gravelly voice that had them listening to him. In no time, he had them hooked up, but getting them out the door and headed in the right direction wasn't as easily accomplished.

She watched Michael and the puppies walk away. She wasn't sure what to make of him. One moment he could be a little bit grumpy and a bit standoffish, and yet in the next moment, he was taking care of the puppies. Michael Bishop was the most intriguing man she'd ever met. Too bad she wasn't sticking around Kringle Falls long enough to get to know him better.

CHAPTER FIVE

WHAT HAD HE GOTTEN himself into?

Michael had been upset with the mess the puppies made. He couldn't believe something so cute could be so destructive.

But as he walked them through the mudroom and out the back door, they were well-behaved. The husky pup was in the lead. He seemed to be the one in charge, and the other two were happy to follow his lead. It also led Michael to believe that the husky was the one who had come up with the idea to use the pillow for tug-of-war. He'd have to keep a close eye on the little troublemaker.

He recalled the worried look on Candi's face. It was more than worry. It was more like panic. He hated that he'd made her feel that way. After all, it was just a pillow. Right?

Nope. He couldn't sell himself that story. That pillow had meant a lot to him. Maybe it shouldn't. After all, it was just some material sewn together.

But the pillow had been hand embroidered by his late wife. And it was the last place his sweet little boy had laid his head. It was where his son had his last sweet dream. The cracks in Michael's heart throbbed. It felt as though he couldn't catch his breath. The pillow was gone—just like his son and his wife were gone. And now he was all alone.

The husky pup let out a bark. He jumped up. His front paws landed on Michael's pant leg. When he looked down into the pup's blue eyes, he noticed something like emotion in them, but he couldn't make out what it was. He petted the dog's head and then gathered the pups to take them back inside.

After he dried their paws and took off their leashes, they all made their way back to the bedroom. He was surprised to find the room all straightened up. It was as though the mess had never happened. And yet when his gaze moved to the bed, he noticed the pillow with Noah's name on it was missing.

His gaze moved to the white garbage bag. He thought of going and retrieving what was left of the pillow, but what good would that do him? There was nothing he could do with the torn material. He didn't know how to sew.

He had to let it go. Just like he'd had to let go of so much in the past two-plus years. With each thing he relinquished, it felt like Evelyn and Noah were slipping further and further from him.

"It's all cleaned up." Candi knelt down in front of the pups. "And you guys have to behave. You know better than that." She lifted her gaze to meet his. "I'm very sorry about this. I can pay you for the pillow."

He shook his head. "That's not necessary."

"I insist."

He shook his head again. "It was an old pillow. It wasn't worth anything." Of course he wasn't going to tell her it was actually priceless to him. He couldn't talk about the past. "Don't worry about it."

She looked as though she were going to argue the point but then changed her mind. "Well, we should get out of your way."

"You can't go." When her eyes widened with alarm, he regretted his poorly chosen words. "I didn't mean it that way. It's just that you don't have your van, and I'm guessing you don't have anywhere to stay in town."

"I, uh..."

"And the way it's snowing outside, you won't be able to make it far." When her gaze searched his, he realized he was hedging around the words he needed to say. "If you want, you and the pups can spend what's left of the night here."

Relief immediately shone in her eyes. "Thank you. You don't know how much this means."

He glanced around the room to make sure there weren't any other mementos that he needed to move away from the pups' sharp teeth. He didn't see anything to move. "You and the pups can stay in this room."

She glanced around. "Are you sure?"

He nodded. "I'll get you a pillow. Do you need something to sleep in?"

She glanced down at the scrubs from the hospital. "No. This is okay."

"Are you sure?"

She nodded. "But thank you for the offer."

"Okay. I'll be back with that pillow."

He headed for the stairs to the second floor. He wasn't used to having guests. His wife would have known what to say or offer. And then it dawned on him that Candi probably needed something to eat.

As he took the stairs two at a time, he searched his memory for what food was in the fridge. There was some pizza in there. And some eggs and toast. In the pantry, he had some cans of soup. He made a mental note to pick up some groceries.

He grabbed a pillow from his bed and rushed back down the steps. He didn't know what he expected when he returned to the guest room, but it wasn't to find Candi sitting in the middle of the floor with the puppies lying around her. Somehow she'd lulled them into a peaceful existence.

He walked over and placed the pillow on the bed. "Can I get you something to eat?" He named off the food he could recall in the kitchen. After she thanked him but said she didn't have an appetite, he said, "Well, if you get hungry during the night, help yourself to anything you find."

"Thank you."

He started out the door and then turned back to her. "I won't be here when you wake up. I need to be out plowing in a few hours. But don't worry. I'll put in a call to get your van towed."

"I'm sorry to be such a bother."

"I'm just glad I saw your tracks. That road doesn't get much traffic, especially in this sort of weather." He hesitated in the doorway as he watched her run her hand over the husky's belly. When her gaze rose to meet his, he realized there was no reason for him to linger. "Good night."

"Night."

He turned to walk away. He hadn't taken more than two steps when he noticed the husky pup had run over to him. Michael stopped and bent down to pick up the pup, which wasn't tiny but he wasn't full grown either. Once he straightened with the pup in his arms, he was thanked with a big wet kiss.

For the first time that evening, he smiled. Maybe this pup wasn't so bad. "You are sleeping here."

He turned back and retraced his steps. He handed the puppy back to Candi. She held him as Michael once more walked away. The puppy let out loud barks, as though saying he didn't want to stay with Candi. But that was where he had to stay. After all, he wasn't going to adopt a dog. *No way.* He had this single, bachelor, answer-to-no-one lifestyle under control.

He made it upstairs and only then remembered that he hadn't eaten. But he didn't have an appetite either. He told himself it was the lateness of the hour and that it had nothing to do with stirring up embers of the past.

After setting the alarm on his phone to go off at 5:00 a.m., he climbed into bed. His mind was racing. He kept replaying the events that had led him to bringing home a beautiful stranger and three ornery puppies.

They were very fortunate that things had turned out as they had. Because if he hadn't decided to turn around where he had, if he hadn't caught sight of those tracks, if he hadn't followed them...

He stopped his troubling thoughts. Everything was okay. And tomorrow Candi and her puppies would be someone else's problem. At last, he drifted off into an exhausted slumber.

It seemed as if he'd just closed his eyes for a moment when the blare of the alarm drew him from a deep, dreamless slumber. His eyes weren't even open yet when he realized something wasn't quite right. He felt something warm snuggled up to his chest.

His eyes fluttered open. In the soft glow from the clock next to his bed, he made out the image of a puppy all curled up. What had she called him? It took a moment, and then he recalled the name: Tank.

Well, it appeared Candi had lost one of her charges. How hard was it to keep track of three puppies? Apparently it was harder than he imagined.

At least this time, Tank was just sleeping and not destroying anything. The little guy's chest rose and fell in an even rhythm. He was sound asleep. Michael knew that as soon as he moved, it would wake Tank, but he didn't have a choice. The roads wouldn't clear themselves.

He rolled out of bed. To his surprise, the pup lifted his head, looked at him, and then went back to sleep as though this were nothing new, and he belonged in the bed. Michael gave a shake of his head as he headed off to the shower.

When Michael was dressed and ready to go, Tank leapt out of bed and moved to his side. Michael looked down at him. "And where do you think you're going?"

A low-pitch bark was Tank's response.

Michael shook his head and couldn't help but smile. "You are definitely something else. And I really appreciate that you didn't destroy any more of my house last night. Now I have to go to work."

"Bark. Bark."

"I suppose I have a moment to take you outside. But you have to make it fast." He started down the stairs. Tank was hot on his heels.

Michael knew he should put the pup on a leash, but that would mean waking Candi to get the leash from her room. He didn't want to disturb her after the evening she'd had. Besides, it was snowing. And with the mounting snow, there was nowhere for the pup to run.

Michael slipped on his boots and coat, which were next to the back door. He flipped on the back light and opened the door. The pup rushed between him and the door and into the falling snow. While Tank took care of business in the area that Michael had previously shoveled, Michael watched as the snow came down fast. If the wind kicked up, there would be whiteout conditions. That would be bad. Very bad.

When he turned back to Tank, the little guy was running through the snow. He jumped in it. He rolled in it. He appeared to be having a grand time.

Michael hated to disturb Tank, but if he didn't get moving, he would be late. And though he was the boss, it didn't mean he didn't have to follow the rules.

"Tank, come," Michael said sternly so the pup would know he meant business.

Tank straightened and stared at Michael. If a puppy could talk, in that moment Michael knew what he would say: *Are you serious? You want me to give up all of this wonderful snow?*

"Tank, come. Now."

Tank shook off a layer of snow and then bounded through the snow until he was next to Michael. Side by side they walked into the house.

After Michael dried off the puppy, he took him to Candi's room. He hated to wake her up, but he didn't trust Tank to roam freely through the house without supervision. When they reached her room, he was relieved to find her door was cracked open.

He scooted Tank into the room and then quietly yanked on the door handle until the latch clicked into place. He could hear the little guy whimpering on the other side of the door. He hoped Tank wouldn't wake Candi or the other puppies, but he had to get going.

He headed for the mudroom. He was starting to think it was never going to stop snowing. It had been coming down now for almost twenty-four hours straight. At least Candi and the puppies would be safe and warm.

After leaving Candi a brief note, he put on his snowsuit and boots. He grabbed his helmet and headed out the door. With all of the snow, he'd left his pickup in the driveway. Today, he was taking his snowmobile.

He'd bought it for occasions like this, but honestly that had just been an excuse to ease his guilt over spending so much money on it. He loved to ride it. When it was just him on the back of it, gliding over the snow for the briefest of moments, that was all that mattered.

He would let go of his grief, his torment, and just be one with the machine. He wanted that release on this snowy chaotic morning, but as he climbed onto the snowmobile and started it up, all he could see was the beautiful stranger with those emerald green eyes.

When was the snow ever going to stop?

Candi awoke to find a note on the kitchen island from Michael. He'd told her to make herself at home. It was super sweet of him.

As she glanced out the kitchen window at the fast-falling snow, she noticed his red pickup was in the driveaway. She wondered how he'd gotten to work. Maybe a co-worker had picked him up?

She poured a cup of coffee, to which she added milk and sugar. She carried it to the living room and turned on the television. There was a lot of news about the roads in Vermont being shut down except for emergency personnel. They certainly didn't have to worry about her going anywhere any time soon. She'd already had her own terrifying moment in the snow. She wasn't looking forward to a repeat.

And then there was the fact that she still wasn't able to call Bob or her contact in Maine. They must be worried by now. And yet with this storm, there was no way to reach the van that held her phone.

But as morning gave way to a snowy afternoon, she wondered when Michael would be home. She couldn't just sit around. It wasn't in her nature to do nothing.

So, she got busy. She washed her still-wet clothes from the accident. And since Michael had some dirty laundry, she did those too. And then she moved to the kitchen. She decided he might appreciate coming home to a hot meal. It was the least she could do to thank him for going out of his way to help her.

She searched the fridge and the pantry. Her options were limited without being able to run to the market. In the end, she settled on preparing a baked pasta casserole. She slipped it into the oven and set the timer.

She kept a close eye on the puppies. She didn't need them to ruin anything else. As it was, she knew Michael was anxious for them to leave. Not that she could blame him. Having a stranger and three lively puppies under his roof was most certainly unexpected.

The one thing that stood out to her was that he didn't have any holiday decorations up. She wondered if the lack of holiday cheer was because he lived alone.

Maybe she could do something to give the place a little bit of holiday cheer. But how? She walked through the living room, dining room, and kitchen. She didn't know what exactly she was looking for, but she kept hoping she'd get an idea of a way to bring him a little bit of holiday cheer.

She wondered if she looked around the upstairs if she would find boxes of decorations. Her gaze moved to the stairs. *Nope.* She wasn't going up there.

Instead, she returned to the kitchen. Maybe she could bake him a holly jolly treat. The more she thought about it, the more she liked the idea. After all, the oven was already hot, and the casserole was almost finished.

She searched the cabinets, taking a mental inventory of the available supplies. He only had the basics, but that was all she needed to make some sugar cookies.

"Bark! Bark!"

She glanced down to see Tank stroll into the kitchen with Odie and Tater Tot right behind him.

They looked expectantly at her. She knew that look. They needed to go outside.

"You guys have terrible timing. I was just about to make cookies." When she looked into their eyes, she felt her irritation melt away. "Come on."

She put on her boots and her coat. When she opened the door, they were met with at least six inches of new snow. Thankfully, Michael had left a shovel next to the door.

Odie and Tater Tot stayed by the doorway, away from the mounting snow. However, Tank bounded into the snow. She worried that he'd get into the deep snow. She called to him, but he ignored her as he continued to run and jump. He was the happiest she'd ever seen him as he rolled in the snow. If a dog could smile, he would be grinning.

Less than ten minutes later, after a fight with Tank, they were back inside. The dogs were dried off and curled up on the kitchen rugs to take a nap. She noticed when they were asleep, they looked so angelic. She would keep all three of them if she could, but since she lost her teaching job this past summer due to downsizing, she was struggling to take care of herself. Besides, her apartment didn't allow dogs.

But she didn't have time to worry about any of that now. She had cookies to bake for Michael. Just then the buzzer went off on the dryer. And she also had clothes to fold.

CHAPTER SIX

H E HAD BEEN GONE longer than he'd planned.

Michael maneuvered the snowmobile toward his house. The snow had momentarily stopped after dumping twelve inches on them since last night. However, the sky was still heavy with clouds. It was only three thirty in the afternoon, but it was already getting dark out.

He put the snowmobile away and headed for the house. As he approached the side door, he noticed the lights were on inside. In that instant, he imagined that his wife, Evelyn, was in the kitchen preparing dinner while his four-year-old son, Noah, was playing on the floor with his collection of toy trucks.

It'd been more than two years since the deadly car accident. In some ways it seemed like so much longer since he'd seen them, and yet in other ways, if he were to close his eyes, he could still hear his son's voice asking him to take him sledding.

Michael gave himself a mental shake. As he crossed the driveway, he noticed a shoveled path that led to the front door. Candi had done that for him? The thoughtful gesture touched him.

He kept going until he reached the side door that led to the mudroom. He opened the door and barely stepped inside before he was surrounded by three dogs, who were barking at him.

"Quiet!" Candi stepped up behind them and clapped her hands to get their attention.

The two smaller dogs retreated to her side, but Tank moved toward Michael. It took a few quick and calculated moves to navigate around the dog, close the door, and not trip over Tank, who wouldn't move.

For a moment, Michael couldn't speak. He was caught off guard by having someone there to greet him. There was the aroma of tomatoes and oregano in the air. She'd made him dinner? He'd forgotten how good it felt to come home to someone.

As soon as the thought crossed his mind, he halted it. Candi wasn't there for him. She was only in his house because her van had gone down over the embankment. End of story.

Tank stayed by his side as Michael took off his coat and boots. The pup looked so eager to please him that Michael found himself reaching out and petting the little guy. Tank's tail rapidly swished back and forth.

When Michael moved toward the kitchen, he noticed another scent. It was much gentler. He inhaled deeper. It smelled like—like Christmas. He turned to Candi. It was then he noticed a smudge of something white on her cheek.

He wasn't sure what to ask first. "What do I smell?"

"Do you like it?" Her gaze searched his.

He didn't know how to respond. A few years ago, he would have told her he liked it a lot. Now, the cinnamon and clove scent reminded him of ghosts from Christmases past. Grief welled up in his chest, momentarily stealing his breath.

"What is it?" His voice came out gruffer than he intended.

The hopeful look on her face fell. "I'm sorry. I thought you might like it. It's just some spices simmering on the stove. I... I'll go get rid of it." She turned and walked away.

He hadn't meant to hurt her feelings. It was just the rush of memories that collided within him had stirred up the pain of loss. But none of that was her fault.

"Candi, wait."

She stopped, but she didn't turn around. He was once again hit with guilt. He didn't want to take his problems out on her.

"I... I like it." It was the truth. It was a pleasant scent. He just had to somehow disentangle the memories from the pleasant scent. Was that even possible?

Candi slowly turned to him. For a moment, she didn't say anything. Her gaze searched his, as though she were trying to figure out if he was telling her the truth.

As the silence ensued, his gaze stumbled across the white smudge on her cheek. "What is on your cheek?"

Her left hand lifted to her face.

"No." He shook his head. "The other side."

Her hand moved and rubbed away the white smudge. "It's probably flour."

"Flour?" Now he was totally intrigued. "Sounds like you've been busy."

"I was." She turned and walked toward the kitchen island.

He followed, curious to see what she'd been up to. When she moved aside, he saw the island was covered with decorated sugar cookies. There were stars, wreaths, and snowmen. They had been painstakingly painted with frosting. Attention had been paid to the details. And he was utterly impressed.

He walked closer to examine them. "You did all of this?" When she nodded, he said, "You're very talented."

"Would you like to be my taste-tester?"

He looked over the few dozen cookies, searching for a cookie that was flawed. It was not an easy task. And then at last he found a reindeer with a broken leg.

He picked it up. "I feel guilty for eating one."

"Why?"

"Because you put so much effort into each of them."

She shrugged. "I made them to be eaten. I just hope they taste as good as they look."

He stared down at the cookie in his hand. "If they taste even half as good as they look, they'll be amazing." And then he took a bite of the cookie. All of its buttery goodness practically melted on his tongue. It was sweet but not too sweet. It was firm but not too firm.

Once again, he was swept up in the past. Evelyn wasn't a baker. She would bring home cookies from the bakery and plate them like they were her own creations. The memories were like a sucker punch to the gut.

"You don't like it?" The corners of Candi's lips lowered into a frown as disappointment shone in her eyes.

"No." Then he realized that had come out wrong. "I mean, no, I do like it."

Her brows rose. "You do?"

He nodded. "This might be the best cookie I've ever eaten. Are you a professional baker?"

She shook her head. "I was a teacher. Elementary school."

"Was?" The word slipped past his lips before he could stop it.

She nodded. "I was a kindergarten teacher until this past summer when the school board restructured things, and due to downsizing, my job was eliminated."

He could hear the pain in her voice. "I'm sorry." Tank pawed at his pant leg. "And now you're working at an animal shelter?"

"Kind of. I'm doing substitute teaching while I look for a permanent position. I've been volunteering at the animal shelter for the past five or so years, but the owner is not in good health so he's shutting the place down. These were the last three puppies that needed a home. I'm supposed to deliver them to a shelter in Maine, where they will hopefully find their forever home. I really need to contact the shelter. They'll start to think I'm not coming."

He reached into his pocket and pulled out his phone. He held it out to her. "You can use my phone."

"Thank you. But I don't remember the woman's name or number. It's all on my phone." She looked expectantly at him. "Can we go get the van now?"

He rubbed the back of his neck. "About that... I talked to Stan." Seeing the confusion in her eyes, he said, "Stan owns the garage in town. He won't be able to recover the van until tomorrow. At the earliest. No one wants to risk it in the dark."

Candi glanced toward the window as though she didn't realize it was dark out already. "Oh. Yes. Right."

He could tell she was doing her best to hide her disappointment, but it was there in her big green eyes. "I'm sorry. I know people must be worried about you. Are you sure you don't know anyone you can call?"

"I guess I shouldn't rely on my cell phone so much. I've been giving it a lot of thought, and I think I know my friend's number."

He retrieved his phone. "Here."

He stepped out of the room to give her some privacy. In the living room, he found the pups all stretched out, taking a nap. They looked so innocent when they were sleeping, but he knew that would all change when they woke up, recharged and ready to play.

When he heard footsteps behind him, he turned. "Did you reach your friend?"

"Yes. She's going to try and reach Bob for me."

"That's good. I'm sure he's worried."

She held the phone out to him. When he went to take it from her, their fingers brushed. It was as though static electricity arced between them. For a moment, neither of them moved. And then the tingle pulsed up his arm and settled in his chest, making his heart beat faster.

He pulled his hand away but not before his gaze momentarily strayed to her rosy lips. He wondered what it would be like to kiss her.

The thought startled him. He turned away, hoping she didn't notice the direction his thoughts had taken. It felt as the past and present were crashing in on him, pulling him in two different directions. For so long, he'd clung to the past like a drowning man clinging to a life preserver, but now he felt himself being drawn to the present. A wave of conflicting emotions washed over him.

"Are you hungry?" Her voice drew him from his troubled thoughts.

Grateful that she hadn't called him out on staring at her lips, he turned to her and said, "As a matter of fact, I am."

"Good. Because I made you dinner."

He followed her back into the kitchen. She opened the oven and pulled out the still-warm casserole. She placed it on a couple of hot pads on the island. "I hope you like this."

He moved closer and inhaled. "I don't know what it is, but it smells delicious."

A smile pulled at the corners of her lips. "I'll get you a plate."

He was touched. Michael couldn't remember the last time someone had prepared him a meal—other than the numerous casseroles the whole town had gotten together to send over when his family died. His freezer had been full for the longest time. Did they have any idea how long it took one person to eat that much food?

And to make matters worse, he hadn't had any appetite for the longest time. He lost so much weight in those first few months that if it weren't for a belt, his pants never would have stayed up. He never thought he'd be able to crawl back from that dark place.

It had been a matter of getting through one hour at a time and then one day at a time. There wasn't one particular point where suddenly his life was right again, because that never happened. It never would.

He'd just very slowly learned how to live with the giant gaping cracks in his heart. He didn't think they would ever heal. And in some ways, he didn't want them to. They were a link back to Evelyn and Noah.

Still, having Candi and the dogs there was a nice distraction. And that realization surprised him. Part of him felt guilty for enjoying another woman's company. And the other part of him was starving for the companionship—for a moment to feel...well, to feel normal or at least as close to it as he could get.

Michael inhaled the aroma of oregano, basil, and tomatoes. Whatever Candi had prepared for dinner was making his mouth water in anticipation.

Beep.

He knew that sound. He turned to Candi. "Do you have something in the dryer?"

Her eyes widened with worry. "I do. I'm sorry. I should have asked before using it."

"No. It's fine. When I left you that note and told you to feel at home, I meant it."

"Thanks. You've been so generous. I'll just go grab the clothes so they don't wrinkle." She rushed off to the laundry room, which was situated just off the kitchen.

Realizing he had a stack of dirty clothes that he needed to run through the wash, he followed her. "I just need to do a load." He glanced to the bin where he kept his dirty clothes, but it was empty. How could that be? And then he glanced over at Candi as she pulled a pair of his jeans from the dryer. "You washed my clothes?"

She shrugged. "It seemed like the right thing to do. You know, since you've been so nice to me and the three musketeers."

He took the jeans from her. "I'll fold them."

She looked hesitant. "I can do it."

"No. They're my clothes, I'll do it." He knew he was being ridiculous. Lots of people would be excited to have someone come in and do so much for them.

But it felt too cozy for him. The last woman to fold his clothes had been Evelyn. He just wasn't ready for someone else to fill that role—even if it was just a friendly gesture.

Candi kept reminding him of how things used to be. She showed him how easy it would be to move on—if he would just let himself. But he couldn't do it. He couldn't let go of the past like Evelyn and Noah never existed.

Being around Candi reminded him that there was still life to live—his life to live. But was he ready for that? The question niggled at the back of his mind as he folded the rest of his clothes.

Afterward, Michael entered the kitchen to find Candi washing dishes. "I'm sorry. I shouldn't have made a big deal out of the laundry. I... I overreacted."

She turned to him. Her questioning gaze met his, but she remained quiet.

He raked his fingers through his hair. "It's been a long time since I had someone do all of these things for me. It's kind of you. I'm just not used to it."

She nodded. "I understand. In my effort to thank you for helping us, I overstepped. I'm sorry too."

After a moment, she asked, "Would you still like to eat?"

"Yes. That would be nice." Michael put a couple of plates and some silverware on the kitchen table. In no time, they were seated with the dogs sitting close by, waiting to catch any scraps that might fall from the table.

"You have a really beautiful home," Candi said.

He lifted his gaze and looked around. Once upon a time, the kitchen had been the hub of activity. This table had been where Noah learned his ABCs and numbers. It was where he and Evelyn would sit long after dinner was over, talking about their days.

Now, there was just him.

"I can't really take credit for anything. My wife did all of the decorating."

Her eyes widened in surprise. "She has great taste."

"*Had* great taste," he corrected. "She, uh..." He swallowed hard, trying to keep the emotion out of his voice. And yet when he spoke again, his voice cracked with emotion. "She passed away a couple of years ago."

"I'm so sorry." Candi fingered her utensils as though unsure what to say.

The rest of their meal was quiet. He tried to think of something to talk about, but nothing sounded right in his mind. He told himself it was best if they didn't get too close—didn't learn too much about each other. But he couldn't deny he was curious about her.

When the meal was over and it was time to clean up, he offered to take care of everything, but she insisted on helping. In the end, she washed the items that didn't go in the dishwasher, and he dried them.

The awkward silence was going on too long. Perhaps it wouldn't hurt to know more about her. "Have you always lived in Ohio?"

"Uh..." She glanced over at him. Surprise shone in her eyes. "Yes."

"Do you have a lot of family?"

She shook her head. "I just have an aunt, but we're not close at all. Years ago, my mother and her had some sort of falling out. To be honest, I don't know what it was about, but they never spoke again. I can't imagine never speaking to a sibling again, but maybe that's because I never had one." She was quiet for a moment as though contemplating what it would be like to have a brother or a sister. "Anyway my aunt didn't even show up at my mother's funeral. So, for practical purposes, I don't have any family. At least none that mean anything to me."

"That's too bad."

"Do you have family here in town?"

He nodded. "I have a lot of family here. There are my parents and my three brothers. I have an aunt, uncle, and three cousins."

"Are you all close?"

He nodded. "We get together for holidays and birthdays."

"Must be nice. I miss my parents. My dad died when I was a kid, and my mother passed a few years ago."

He felt bad for her being all alone. Of course, he was alone most of the time, but that was due to his own choice. After he lost Evelyn and Noah, it was easier for him to be alone. He didn't have to put a smile on his face when he felt miserable. He didn't have to make excuses for losing track of a conversation because his thoughts meandered to memories of Evelyn and Noah.

Maybe it was time to change the conversation. "You must be anxious to get home."

She shrugged. "With the animal shelter shutting down, I don't really have any plans for the holiday." She rinsed a plate and placed it in the drainer. She glanced at him. "Please, don't go thinking that I'm pathetic and don't have a life. I do. I have friends. It's just that I haven't made any firm plans for the holiday."

He nodded. "I'd like to say that I don't have any firm plans, but my mother would strongly disagree with that statement."

Candi smiled. "Sounds like you are close."

He nodded. "Close enough. Of course, if it was up to my mother, I'd be eating dinner at her house every evening."

"I take it that's not your style?"

Michael shook his head. "My mother is well-meaning, but she hovers if you let her. I just need my own space."

Just then Odie moved to the back door and whined. Michael knew what that meant. He set aside the drying towel. "I'll take them out."

"You don't have to. I can do it."

"It's okay. The area probably needs to be shoveled again." He moved to the door and put on his coat and boots. The puppies all fought to get out the door at the same time. They stumbled over each other. In the end, Tank got out the door first. Michael was not surprised. Tank appeared to take his position as the leader of the group seriously.

Michael shoveled out a spot for the pups, while Tank jumped into the higher snow. Michael smiled and shook his head. The little fellow definitely enjoyed the snow. He'd do well living in Vermont.

He glanced over at the other two pups. They were not as fond of the white stuff. They did their business and then hustled back to the door.

In the end, he had to take the two pups in first and dry them off while Tank continued to romp around in the snow. When he saw Michael, he rushed toward him. Tank leapt up. His snow-covered paws landed on Michael's pant leg.

Michael ran a gloved hand over the dog's head. "Are you having fun?"

As if Tank could understand him, he barked. Then he got down and ran back into the deep snow. All the while his tail swished back and forth. Michael wasn't comfortable with Tank playing in the deep snow, because it was well over the puppy's head. So Michael called Tank, and to his surprise, the pup came running to him.

Michael found the little guy was growing on him. Not that he was thinking of adopting him. Michael reassured himself that he was fine on his own.

But that wasn't the real truth, and he knew it. He couldn't risk letting someone, not even a rambunctious puppy, into his heart. He'd barely survived the loss of his wife and son. He couldn't go through something like that again.

CHAPTER SEVEN

THE SECOND LOAD OF laundry was in the dryer.

The dishes had been washed and put away. And the Christmas cookies were arranged neatly on the platter.

Candi didn't know what else to do. She checked the time. It was only a little after six. It was far too early to go to bed.

If she were at her apartment, she'd probably turn on the television and do some knitting. She was working on a blanket to give her friend Stacy for Christmas. Candi still had a ways to go before it was finished. She should have brought it with her. But then again, she didn't think she'd have any spare time to work on it.

Michael had disappeared without a word. She wondered where he'd gone. She glanced toward the mudroom and noticed his coat and boots were missing. Maybe he'd driven into town.

She turned to the living room. Perhaps she'd check out what was on television. She grabbed the remote and plunked down onto the couch. To her surprise, he had some premium stations. She found a Christmas movie. Grabbing a blanket from the back of the couch, she made herself comfortable.

The pups, one by one, begged to join her. And soon the couch held her with Tank lying next to her while Odie and Tater Tot stretched out on her other side. She made an effort to fuss over each of them. They were so easy to love that she was surprised they hadn't found their forever homes yet.

One day she planned to adopt a dog of her own. Sadly, this wasn't that day. She always told herself that she'd pick the pup that everyone at the shelter would skip over—the pup with a big heart who wasn't perfect.

But the more time she spent with the three musketeers, the more attached she became to them. It was going to be hard to give them up when she finally reached Maine, but it was for the best. She couldn't keep one dog, much less three of them. No matter how cute she found them.

Midway through the movie, there was a commercial break. She had a craving for a cookie. When she stood, the dogs hopped down. They raced ahead of her toward the kitchen and sat by the back door.

"Not again." She really didn't want to bundle up and go out in the cold. Again.

"Bark. Bark." Tank looked expectantly at her.

She was quite certain he just wanted to go out and play in the snow some more. But when the other two barked, she figured theirs was a genuine need.

She sighed as she put on her boots and then shrugged on her coat. She'd noticed that Michael hadn't been using the leashes for the dogs. She supposed with all of the snow that had fallen there wasn't anywhere they could go, but she wasn't taking any chances. Besides it was easier to coral Tank when he was leashed.

They trudged out into the cold. Candi slouched down into her coat, trying to hide from the wind. A gust of wind picked up the top layer of snow, swirled it around, and then swept it away. By morning, there were going to be a lot of snow drifts in the area.

Once the wind died down, she noticed there were lights on in the garage. That must be where Michael had disappeared to.

When the dogs finished their business, she directed them toward the garage. Maybe Michael had cleared out of the house to give her some space. She felt bad about chasing him out of his own home. She could invite him to watch the movie with her. She would even start it over from the beginning for him.

She hesitated outside the door. Should she bother him? Then, deciding she was being silly, she knocked on the door.

"Come in." Michael's voice sounded from inside.

She opened the door, not sure what to expect. It certainly wasn't to find Michael at a workbench covered with small pieces of wood. *So, the plowman has a hobby? Interesting.*

She approached him. "Hi. I... I just wanted to let you know that I'm going to watch a holiday movie, if you want to join me."

"Is it the one with Bruce Willis?"

She knew exactly what movie he was referring to. "That's not a Christmas movie."

"Yes, it is."

"No, it isn't."

He rolled his eyes. "Looks like we'll have to agree to disagree."

She was fine with that because there was nothing he could say to change her mind about the movie. Instead, she checked out the pieces of wood on the table. "What are you doing?"

"I'm cutting ornaments."

"Really?" She didn't know why that surprised her so much. Maybe it was because there weren't any holiday decorations in the house.

"Don't look so shocked." He turned back to the round slices of a branch he'd just cut. He picked one up. "It needs to be sanded. A hole drilled in the top for the ribbon. And then it'll be painted."

She accepted the piece of wood and looked at it. "You do all of it, including the painting?"

Michael nodded. "My grandfather started the tradition. And then my father took over. Now that my father's arthritis is so bad, I've taken over."

She glanced around and found what looked to be dozens of them stacked on a table behind her. "Wow! That's a lot of ornaments."

"Yes. I still have a long way to go."

"Could you use some help?"

He arched a brow. "You want to paint ornaments?"

"Sure. It's not like I have anything to do. By the way, what do you do with them?"

"Every Christmas Eve my parents dress up like Santa and Mrs. Claus and they visit the local hospital. They hand them out to the patients."

"Aw... That's so touching. It's a wonderful family tradition. My family never did anything like that."

Luckily, the workshop was heated by a wood-burning stove. Michael made a spot for the dogs near the stove, and then he helped her get situated at the work table. And for the next few hours, she painted while he sanded the little wooden discs and drilled a hole for the red satin ribbon.

She loved that she was getting to see these different sides of Michael. The more she got to know about him, the more she wanted to know.

Beep-beep-beep.

Michael groaned. It was his day off.

Beep-beep-beep.

And he'd forgotten to turn off the alarm on his phone.

He reached over to the end table, and at last his fingers connected with his phone. He kept pressing on the phone's face until silence settled over the room once more.

He rolled over and snuggled down under the duvet. He loved that it was cool in the room, but it was cozy under the covers. He was just about to drift off again, when there was something wet against his cheek.

His eyes flew open. Right in his face was Tank. He closed his eyes again. This wasn't happening. It was a dream. Had to be.

The pup sighed. Michael inhaled the strong scent of dog breath. *Ugh!*

With a groan, he rolled over in the other direction. That's when he felt four little feet stomp over his ribs. The dog was not light. There was another lick to his other cheek.

Michael opened his eyes again. "How did you get up here?"

"Bark. Bark."

"Shh... We don't want to wake everyone up. You do realize it's still dark out, and I was really hoping to sleep until sun up."

Tank whined.

"Fine. Let's go."

Tank didn't have to be told twice. He bounded off the bed and headed for the door. Michael wasn't that fast. He had to throw on his jeans and a sweatshirt.

A few minutes later, Tank had taken care of business, and for once the little guy wasn't interested in playing in the snow. That was fine with Michael. He had plans to go back to sleep, even if it was only for an hour.

When he opened the kitchen door, Tank rushed inside. By the time Michael got his coat off, the dog had disappeared. Michael didn't even have a chance to dry him off. *Oh, well.*

Michael quietly climbed the stairs, not wanting to wake Candi or the other dogs. When at last he was ready to crawl back into his comfy bed, he found Tank was in his spot. Michael once more groaned. Tank chose to ignore him as he was all curled up on the sheets with his head on Michael's pillow. This wasn't happening. Michael gave a gentle push to Tank's back, but the stubborn dog wouldn't move. *Seriously?*

With a huff, Michael walked around to the other side of the bed and climbed in. This side wasn't as comfortable. The pillows weren't the same. The lumps in the mattress weren't in the right places.

He flipped and flopped around, trying to get comfortable. It didn't bother Tank. The dog was out to the world and to top it off, Tank snored. *Unbelievable.*

At last, Michael got as comfortable as he was going to get. His breathing evened out, and he was in that place between reality and dreamland.

Buzz. Buzz.

His phone startled him out of his slumber. It was a conspiracy to keep him from sleeping. He wasn't answering it. If it was work, they could deal with the problem just this once. He rolled over and pulled up the covers.

Thunk!

His still-ringing phone had vibrated itself off the edge of the nightstand and landed on the floor. Michael gave up. That was it. He was done. There would be no more sleep.

He threw back the covers and got out of bed. He picked up the phone on what must have been the last ring before it switched to voicemail.

He didn't even look at the caller ID before pressing it to his ear. "What?"

"Michael, is that you?" a male voice asked.

"Yeah. Who is this?"

"It's Stan at the garage. I have some time if you want to see if we can retrieve that van."

He might as well. He glanced over at the dog, who was hogging the bed. It wasn't like he was going to get back to sleep.

"Give me forty-five minutes, and I'll meet you at the garage."

"Sounds good."

They disconnected, and Michael gave Tank one final frown. "Must be nice."

Then Michael headed for the shower. The sooner they retrieved the van, the sooner he would get his house and bed back. Not so long ago that would have sounded good to him, but now he would have to get used to the loneliness once more.

Chapter Eight

"Bark. Bark."

Candi opened her eyes. Both Odie and Tater Tot stood on the bed, staring at her. She'd had a hard time going to sleep the night before. She looked at the window and saw it was still dark out. She didn't need a clock to tell her it was far too early to get out of bed.

She was just about to roll over and go back to sleep when she realized there were only two pups bugging her to get up. The leader of the pack was quiet. Her spidey senses kicked in. *What exactly is Tank up to?*

She opened her eyes and bolted upright. She squinted into the darkness. She didn't see Tank anywhere on the bed. *This is not good.*

She rolled over and turned on the bedside light. Odie and Tater Tot started dancing in excitement on the bed. This was one of their signals when they had to go outside, and then they'd want their breakfast. It was their favorite meal of the day. Well, that wasn't quite true. When she was working at the shelter, she frequently took them out for strolls. A few times they'd stopped at the nearby ice cream shop where she'd gotten them pup cones. They went crazy over them.

She jumped out of bed. The hardwood floor was cold against her bare feet. She ignored the goosebumps that cascaded over her body. She had to find the ringleader.

She rushed around the bed. She made sure to keep her voice low as she didn't want to wake Michael. "Tank, where are you?"

As she turned around, she noticed the bedroom door was cracked open. *Oh no.* She grabbed a throw blanket from the bottom of the bed and wrapped it around her shoulders. With it still being dark out, she tried to remember her way around the house without running into any furniture.

She only went a few steps when she noticed light coming from the kitchen. *Is Michael up? Already?* She hesitated to go in that direction because then she would have to explain why she was awake at that early hour. And yet, she had to find Tank. She didn't even want to imagine what mischief he might get into on his own.

When she stepped into the kitchen, she inhaled the aroma of fresh-brewed coffee. She resisted the draw to the coffeemaker. She glanced around the kitchen. There was no sign of Tank or Michael. Where were they?

"Tank, come." Michael's voice came from the direction of the stairs.

Candi didn't think Tank would listen to Michael. That dog had a mind of his own. Unless Michael had a leash on Tank, he would have to pick up the furbaby and carry him downstairs.

She took a couple steps backward and glanced up the steps in time to see Tank following Michael. Candi's mouth gaped.

Her gaze met Michael's. "How did you do that?"

Michael's brows drew together. "Do what?"

"Get Tank to listen to you."

Michael shrugged. "I just told him to come, and he did."

While Tank ran into the living room with the other two dogs, she said, "He certainly seems happy."

"He should be. He slept in my bed last night." There was a definite grumble in his voice.

Oh no. This was definitely not good. "I'm so sorry. I must not have gotten the bedroom door closed the whole way."

He shook his head. "It's not your fault. I should have told you the door is a little warped and, in the winter, it takes a bit of a push to get the latch to work."

"Oh." It was too late to help her now because today she would get the van back, and soon she'd be on her way to Maine. Still, she worried about the frown on Michael's face. "I hope he didn't keep you up all night."

Michael shook his head. "He didn't keep me up at all. But when my phone went off this morning, he thought it was time to get up and play. He licked my face."

The more Michael frowned, the harder it was to hold back her smile. "He was just giving you a kiss."

"I could do without those types of kisses."

The next thing she knew, she was staring at Michael's lips and wondering what sort of kisser he might be. Would his kisses be sweet and tender? Or would they be heated and sweeping?

She couldn't make up her mind on which it would be. It was then she noticed how close he was standing. If she lifted up on her tiptoes and leaned forward, their lips would meet.

Michael cleared his throat.

Immediately, she stepped back as heat rushed to her face. She'd been busted staring at him. What was wrong with her? She wasn't there to start anything with Michael. Not at all. So, what was she supposed to say to him now?

When Odie and Tater Tot started to fuss at the back door, Michael said, "I'll take them out."

For once, she decided not to argue with him. It was just too early to deal with going out in the cold. "Thank you. I'll get them breakfast, but I really need to go to the store to get them more food."

"Don't worry. We have a pet store in town. You can stop there after you get your van back."

"Is there news about it?"

He nodded. "I just had a call this morning. In fact, I'm leaving to go meet Stan to recover the van."

This was the best news she'd heard in a long time. "Give me ten minutes, and I'll go with you."

He hesitated. "Are you sure? It's really cold out."

Suddenly, she realized he didn't want her to go with him. It probably had something to do with him catching her staring at him. He wasn't interested in her and didn't want to give her the wrong impression. She could understand that. Why had she picked that moment to let her imagination get the best of her?

"It's okay," she said. "I totally understand."

When she turned her back to him, she heard some movement, and then the back door opened, and cold air rushed in before it closed once more. She grabbed the dog bowls from a spot on the counter and filled each with puppy food.

She bent over and put them in their places. Then a thought struck her. In such a short amount of time, they'd already started having routines, such as the placement of the dog bowls. At this rate, she couldn't get the van back soon enough.

And that was why she made a decision. She was going with Michael to get the van whether he liked it or not. She couldn't waste any more time in Kringle Falls. It was time to move on to Maine.

She rushed to her room, grabbed her clothes, and then took the fastest shower of her life. She made sure not to get her hair wet. There was no time to dry it, and out in that cold, wet hair would freeze. The last thing she wanted to do was walk around with icicles hanging from her head.

She threw on the clothes she'd washed the day before. She rushed to the mudroom to put on her boots when she realized she needed to take the pups with her, especially Tank, who appeared to be an escape artist. She didn't need the three musketeers tearing apart any other pillows.

She called them, and for once they all came to her. She attached their leashes, and out the door they went. She saw the white puff of exhaust coming from Michael's truck. She walked faster.

She rushed up the side of the pickup and pulled open the door. Her gaze briefly met Michael's surprised look. She turned away to pick up the puppies and place them in the truck.

"What are you doing?" Agitation laced Michael's voice.

"What does it look like? We're going with you."

"That's not a good idea. The back roads are still in bad condition."

"We'll be fine." After situating the three puppies between them on the bench seat, she put on her seatbelt. When she could still feel Michael frowning at her, she said, "Shouldn't we get going?"

She stared straight ahead as Tater Tot settled on her lap. She petted him while keeping her focus on the snowy scene before them.

After a few moments, Michael put the truck in gear and they set off down the road. She couldn't wait for the van to be back on the road. It was time for her to get on with her journey to Maine. Kringle Falls had been an interesting detour, but it was time to get on with her life.

―*ele*―

This was the moment they'd been waiting for.

Michael stood at the edge of the road and stared down over the snowy embankment. There were four men and two tow trucks working to haul the van up to the roadway. Two men were working the controls on the two winches. The other two men were down the embankment, standing on either side of the van.

To get the van up to the roadway, they had to maneuver it between a handful of trees and lots of overgrown bushes. Candi made sure to stress how important it was for the van not be further damaged during the recovery because she didn't own it. Of course, her plea had been sprinkled with charm and a bit of begging. How could any man deny her anything when she flashed those emerald green eyes at them?

The pups had been left inside his pickup. No one wanted them getting loose and getting hurt. Of course, Tank wasn't happy about the decision and made his displeasure known with his incessant barking. Eventually, he settled down and curled up on Michael's seat.

Michael left the engine running to keep the pups warm. Candi insisted on standing out in the cold with him. She wanted to watch them recover the van. He glanced over at her. She had her gloved hands stuffed into her pockets. The tip of her nose was red as were her cheeks.

He recalled how he'd caught her staring at him back at the house. It caught him off guard. Had she been staring at his mouth? It'd all happened so fast. As soon as she noticed that he'd caught her staring, she'd glanced away. Had she been thinking about kissing him?

The part that bothered him the most was that he wouldn't have minded if she had kissed him. What did that say about him? He hadn't thought about kissing anyone since his wife. He'd never let his thoughts go in that direction. Starting a new relationship was never something he'd considered. He'd loved once; it was enough for him.

And then Candi stumbled into his life. She was full of life and so different from Evelyn, who was quiet and reserved. He always knew where he stood with Evelyn. But with Candi, he felt a little off kilter.

Candi glanced over at him, as though she could tell the direction of his thoughts. He quickly looked away. He was venturing into dangerous territory.

He had to stay focused on getting Candi's vehicle back on the road, and then she would be on her way. Then his life would return to the way it had been before Candi and the three pups had him thinking about all of the things he was missing in his life.

"Hold!" Michael was acting as a spotter. "Move it a foot to the left to miss a tree."

The two lines they had attached to the van allowed them to maneuver the vehicle left and right as needed. The fact that Candi had barreled down over the embankment without hitting any of the trees or large rocks was nothing short of a miracle. He didn't even want to think about what might have happened if the van had gone a little to the left or veered to the right.

When Candi ventured closer to the tow truck to have a better look, Michael said, "Candi, you need to step over here by me. If one of those lines snaps, it's going to be bad."

Her gaze moved from him to the cables, which were under great force. She didn't argue as she moved closer to the pickup. After checking on the pups, she stood quietly beside him as she wrung her hands.

He forced his attention back to the van. It was nearing the top. The recovery had gone smoothly so far. The winches both whined as they spooled up the cables attached to the van. Just a little more, and they'd have it up on the road.

There was a pause as the one tow truck was repositioned for the last pull. It was during this moment that Candi stepped up to him. "What do you think?"

"Candi, don't get too excited about the van being drivable."

"It'll be fine. Just wait and see. Soon we'll be back on the road." Her voice held a positive note.

She certainly seemed anxious enough to get away from him. The thought stung. For the first time since he'd become a widower, his house once more felt like a home. There were sounds of life from the clanging of pots and pans in the kitchen to the lilt of Candi's singing as she folded the laundry. It reminded him that he didn't have to be alone.

And that was why he wasn't ready for her to leave. It had nothing to do with how much he'd come to enjoy her company. And it certainly had nothing to do with her merry trio of troublemakers.

CHAPTER NINE

THIS WAS IT.

They'd finally see the damage.

Candi watched as they adjusted the placement of the tow lines on the van. The men made it all look so easy to drag the van up the embankment, but she knew without their experience that it would have been a disaster.

The snow and ice had caused them countless problems. And yet they were at the final stage as the van teetered near the roadway. Was it too much to hope that once they got the van on the road that she'd be able to drive off in it? *Probably.* But it didn't keep her from wishing.

Her gaze shifted to where Michael was standing. There was a part of her that didn't want to leave Kringle Falls, but the little voice inside her head said if she didn't leave soon that she was going to fall for this tall, dark, and brooding man.

And would that be so bad? *Yes.*

For one, her life was back in Cleveland. She had an apartment and working as a substitute teacher wasn't so bad. Okay. That wasn't the truth, no matter how much she tried to convince herself.

She didn't like it. She craved a reliable work schedule. The longer she was away from teaching, the more she was thinking that maybe it wasn't her calling. But her feelings might change once she found a new position.

For two, Michael wasn't interested in her. He was still in love with his wife. He kept memories of her all around him in that house. There were pictures of them on the bookshelves and mementos strewn from one room to the next. Something told her he'd left everything the way it'd been when his wife and son were alive, as though he were waiting for them to walk back through the door any day now. Her heart ached for him. She couldn't imagine the pain he'd endured.

Candi would have come up with a third reason why leaving sooner rather than later was best, but her thoughts were interrupted when the van crested the side of the road. Excitement flooded her veins. She'd been so worried that she'd totaled Bob's van, but of what she saw so far, it looked to be in pretty good shape. *Not perfect. But better than it could have been.* She would definitely pay for any repairs.

But what she was most excited about was getting her purse and phone back. She would at last be able to make phone calls and let people know she was all right.

When all four wheels of the van were on the asphalt, she rushed forward. She moved too fast, forgetting the road was still icy in places. Her feet hit a patch of ice and then they went out from under her. Her arms stretched out. There was nothing to grab. In an instant, she was careening toward the cold ground.

Before she hit the hard, cold asphalt, a pair of strong hands reached out to her. They caught her under her arms, stopping her descent.

They helped her regain her balance. She spun around to thank her rescuer. But she hadn't anticipated him standing so close. When she turned, she was just a few inches away from Michael. The breath caught in her lungs. She knew she should take a step back, but her feet refused to cooperate.

Instead, she stood there, staring into his dark eyes. They were filled with mystery and something else. It took her a moment, then she realized it was pain.

She longed to take him into her arms and assure him he was going to be all right. But she didn't have that right. And why would he believe her? They hardly knew each other.

Still, what could she say to ease some of his pain? She couldn't think of any appropriate words. But then his gaze lowered and lingered. Was he staring at her lips? Her heart beat faster. So the attraction went both ways. Her heart beat a rap-a-tap-tap in her chest.

When he lowered his head toward hers, the breath caught in her lungs. This was it. He was really going to kiss her. Her eyes fluttered shut.

"Hey, Michael!"

What? No. This isn't happening. Not now.

Candi's eyes snapped open. Michael jerked back. When she looked at him, he turned away. This time she hadn't imagined the moment. It was real. It had happened—well, it'd almost happened.

"Yeah, Stan," Michael said. "What do you need?"

"Thought you mentioned getting something out of the van before we tow it."

That was Candi's cue. She rushed over to the van. "Can't I just drive it?"

Stan shook his head. "Not until we check it out. It might look to be in good shape, but that was quite a wild ride you took down the embankment. Any number of things could be wrong with it."

That wasn't the answer she'd wanted to hear, but she knew Stan was right. She moved to the passenger's side and opened the door. First, she looked in all of the obvious places for her phone: the seat, the dash, and the cup holder. It wasn't in any of those places.

She bent over and searched the floor. A lot of stuff had been shuffled around during the accident. It wasn't until she looked on the driver's side that she found the phone wedged between the seat and the console. The screen had spiderweb cracks through it, but she hoped it would still work. When she tried it, nothing happened. She was faced with a black screen.

"Is everything okay?" Michael stepped up beside her.

"Yeah. I think my phone just needs to be charged." She hoped.

"Are you ready to go?" He seemed anxious for them to be on their way. Was it because he had other things he'd rather be doing? Or, did it have to do with the almost kiss that had been interrupted?

She held up her finger for him to wait. "I need to see if I have more puppy food, and I need my suitcase."

They moved to the back of the van, and she unlocked the doors. She cautiously opened them, worried things would fall out at her. To her relief, nothing was pressing against the doors.

It took her climbing into the back of the van in order to find everything she'd been looking for. It would be nice to have a fresh change of clothes. The hospital scrubs were surprisingly comfortable, but she preferred her jeans and sweaters.

To her disappointment, there wasn't any more puppy food. She'd have to get some on the way back to the house. She hoped Michael wouldn't mind a detour.

With her belongings in hand, she closed the van doors and turned to the tow truck driver. After she relinquished the key to the van, she asked, "How soon can I pick it up?"

The older man rubbed his hand along his salt-and-pepper-colored beard. "I can't really say. It depends on what we find. Can I get your number?" Stan held his phone in his hand in order to enter her number. When she hesitated, he said, "That way I can call you about the van?"

She knew that was why he'd wanted her number, but she worried that her phone might not work. She lifted her phone to look at the cracked black screen. "I'm not sure it's still going to work."

"You can just call me," Michael said. "I'll make sure she gets the message."

Stan nodded his almost bald head as he walked away to work on securing the van to the tow truck.

It wasn't until they were back in Michael's red pickup that she said, "Thank you. I hope after I charge my phone it still works. It was pretty beat up in the accident."

Michael nodded in understanding. "Do you have a charger cord for it?"

"I do. It's in my bag with my clothes." And now there was another topic she needed to cover with him. And she really hated to be more of a burden on him. Still, she didn't have a choice in the matter. "Would it be possible to make a stop on the way back to the house? I desperately need to get some more food for the three musketeers."

"Uh, sure."

"Thank you. I'm so sorry for being such a bother."

"You're not." He reached out to her, as though to pat her hand in reassurance, but before his fingers touched hers, he hesitated and pulled his hand back.

She wanted to believe he didn't see her as a bother. She really did, but it didn't stop her from feeling bad about needing his assistance. "I'm sure the van will be fine." She'd keep her doubts about that statement to herself. "And as soon as it gets a clean bill of health, we'll be on our way."

She glanced over at him and noticed Tank snuggled up against his thigh. The pup had really taken to him. And then she had an idea.

"Tank really likes you," she said.

Michael glanced down as though he wasn't aware the dog was pressed up against him. "He just likes that I let him play in the snow."

She was certain Tank liked that part, but she knew it went beyond that. The dog was very particular about whom he liked. Michael had obviously met the dog's high standards. The question was how fond was Michael of the dog?

"You know he's looking for a home…"

Michael cast her a quick sideways glance. "You surely aren't suggesting I adopt him?"

"Why not? You have that big house. You could use some company."

"No." The one-word response was firm.

She knew she should leave the conversation there, but she was never one to leave things alone when she knew she was right. "But he needs a home."

"I said no."

"He's a really good dog."

"Good?" Michael shook his head. "He's an escape artist. You do realize he's gotten out of your room the last two nights and snuck up to my room. In fact, this morning he stole my side of the bed and my pillow." There was an indignant tone to his voice.

She attempted to smother her amusement. The more Michael talked, the more convinced she was that they belonged together.

Michael gave her a sideways glance. "Stop laughing. This is not funny. The dog has a mind of his own."

She subdued her laughter to say, "And that's a bad thing?"

Michael expelled an exasperated sigh.

She decided to leave the conversation there. She could only push so much, but the conversation wasn't over. Not by a long shot. Sooner or later, he'd realize they belonged together—he and Tank, of course.

As she stared out the window, she noticed they were following a winding river. While there was snow and icicles on the edges of the water, the center was flowing freely. It was so picturesque.

"What's the name of the river?" she asked.

"It's the Kringle River. It flows through the heart of the town."

"Oh. That sounds beautiful."

"If you like that, wait until you see the waterfall in town."

"You have a waterfall in town?"

He nodded. "That's how the town got its name."

"I like this town already, and I haven't seen much of it yet." Her hand ran over Tater Tot's back as he slept.

"Well, you're about to. Because this is the edge of town."

She stared out the window at the big old stately homes. Though they had weathered many years, they had been lovingly tended to. Most had big porches, some with porch swings and others with rockers that were just waiting for springtime to arrive.

After a while, he grew quiet. She'd tried a couple of times to make conversation, but Michael would only give her one-word answers at best and at other times a grunt or nod. The silence was deafening. She glanced over at the radio. It looked like an antique, but what else would you expect in an old truck like this.

She wondered if it worked. "Do you mind if I turn on the radio?"

"No."

She reached for the knob and turned. It clicked. She stopped, wondering if she'd broken it, but then the music came on. It was very faint. She turned the knob some more, and the music grew louder.

It was country music. And though she liked it, she was in the mood for something more festive. "Can I change the station?"

He glanced over at her. "You don't have to keep asking. Feel free to put on whatever you like."

And so she turned the other dial, scrolling down through the various stations. At last, she came across a station that was playing Christmas tunes. "I'll Be Home For Christmas" played, and she started to think about her lonely apartment in Cleveland. There was no one special waiting for her. The thought deflated her mood.

This Christmas she would get together with some friends for Christmas Eve. For Christmas day, she'd probably stay home. Bob would call and insist she come over to his place to celebrate with his friends.

A new song started to play. At first, she didn't recognize it, and then it dawned on her. It was "All I Want For Christmas Is You." Her gaze moved to Michael. Was he paying attention to the song?

Her instinct was to reach out and change the radio station, but she hesitated. If he was listening to the words of the song, would he read something into her need to change stations? She let the song play as she stared out the window.

CHAPTER TEN

B *EEP. BEEP. BEEP.*

"The National Weather Service in Burlington, Vermont, has issued a Severe Winter Storm Warning for Addison County, Bennington County, Caledonia County, Chittenden County, Essex County, Franklin County, Grand Isle County..."

"That includes us." Michael spoke over the radio. "Looks like Mother Nature isn't done dumping snow on us just yet."

The weather alert continued, "The severe winter storm warning is in effect until six p.m. Thursday. The winter storm is capable of producing winds of at least thirty-five miles per hour. Visibility will be reduced to less than a quarter mile. Whiteouts are to be expected. This storm system is expected to produce up to six inches of snow. The storm is currently located in New York and moving northeast at twelve miles per hour..."

Michael turned off the radio.

"Hey, what did you do that for?"

"Because we heard everything we needed to know. Besides, it's not like you can go anywhere just yet." Michael reached over the snoozing dogs to lay his hand over hers. He gave her a reassuring squeeze. "Everything is going to be all right. You and the puppies are safe. That's the most important part."

Where his hand touched hers, it felt as though static electricity arced between them. The sensation sent a wave of goosebumps over her flesh. The reaction was unexpected and intense. She told herself she was worked up about the storm warning, and it had nothing to do with Michael's hand on hers.

She noticed how his hand lingered longer than necessary. Her gaze lowered to where they were touching. She should move her hand, but she didn't want to. Not yet.

Instead, she averted her gaze to the lazy river flowing through the valley. "I just feel like I'm letting people down."

"You had an accident. I'm sure they'll understand." As though he remembered his hand was still resting on hers, he moved it.

Immediately, she noticed the distinct coldness where he was touching her just a moment ago. She missed the warmth of his touch, but she resisted the urge to reach out to him. "I guess. I just wish my phone was working."

"Sorry you can't charge it in here. This truck was around long before cell phones."

"Your grandfather must have thought highly of you to leave it to you."

"Or he figured I was the only one in the family who knew how to keep it running."

She glanced around at the interior, noticing that nothing looked worn out. Michael had taken loving care of it. "Have you done much work on it?"

Michael nodded. "After all of this time, I don't think there's a part of the truck that I haven't cleaned, fixed, or replaced."

"I guess your grandfather knew what he was doing when he left it to you."

Michael didn't say anything, but she noticed how his chin lifted ever so slightly, and the slightest of smiles lifted the corners of his lips. Happiness looked good on him. He should definitely smile more often.

Not sure how to keep the conversation going, she asked, "Do you mind if I turn on the music again?"

"I guess not."

She turned the knob and heard the click before the Christmas music came through the truck's speakers. She leaned back against the seat and stared out at the passing scenery. It was then she noticed snowflakes begin to fall.

It appeared they had gotten the forecast right. More snow was on the way. She would be stuck in Kringle Falls until it passed over. It also meant she would be spending more time with Michael. She couldn't deny the idea appealed to her. She enjoyed spending time with him.

And then she had a thought. "I suppose this means I could paint more of those ornaments."

He gave her a quick sideways glance. "You want to?"

She nodded. "I enjoyed it."

"Then it sounds like a plan." He was quiet for a moment before he said, "But first we need to swing by the market and pick up some groceries."

"And the pet store," she reminded him.

"How could I possibly forget? These little ones have quite the appetite."

"That's because they're growing."

"Is that what you think? I think it's just because they need the energy so they can play all of the time." His tone was light and teasing.

If she didn't know better, she'd think the pups were growing on him. Tank was still pressed up against Michael's leg, as though he belonged there, and there was no other place in this world he wanted to be.

The radio crackled. She couldn't tell if it was the distance or the bad weather. Maybe it was a combination of both.

"Deck the Halls" came to an end, and the radio announcer's warm, deep voice came through the speakers. "With another storm on the way, it looks like there's going to be a run on bread and milk. Stay tuned for any weather updates."

An advertisement for a local hardware store played, followed by "Let It Snow." Someone had a strange sense of humor.

She continued to stare out the windshield as the snowflakes grew in size and intensity. With the temperature hovering just below freezing, it wouldn't take long for the roadways to become covered.

When the truck veered away from the river, she was disappointed. She wanted to see Kringle Falls. "Will we be driving past the waterfall?"

He gave her a quick glance. "Curious, huh?"

She nodded. "It must be impressive for an entire town to be named after it. But it's okay. I don't want to take up any more of your time."

He didn't say anything, but at the next intersection, he put on the turn signal and turned to the right—back in the direction of the river. He was taking her to see Kringle Falls. She was touched by the gesture.

She peered out the window at the passing houses all dressed up with strings of unlit lights. There were deflated characters just waiting for evening to settle in and their fans to be plugged in so they could wave at passersby.

She really wanted to see this town in the evening, when it came to life. But she would have to be content with this short tour.

He pointed in the direction of the passenger's window. "Over there is Kringle Falls Park."

She whipped her head around to stare out the window. She couldn't see anything. She sat up taller, hoping it would help her see better. "I don't see it."

"Hang on a moment." He pulled up to a stop sign. Then he made another right turn. "Look out your window as we cross the bridge."

She kept her gaze focused out the window, and then she saw it. It was nothing as grand as Niagara Falls, but it had its own beauty. The water dropped about thirty or forty feet. It was beautiful as the water rushed over the numerous rocks. All too soon they exited the bridge, and the waterfall was out of sight.

"Thank you," she said. "It was beautiful."

"If there wasn't snow on the ground, I'd take you over to the platforms that overlook the falls."

"I would have liked that." She meant it. "But sadly, I'll be gone long before the snow melts."

"Maybe you could stop back sometime." His tone was casual, as though he knew it would never happen, and it was just wishful thinking.

"Maybe." The thought appealed to her more than she was expecting. "We'll see."

The layer of snow that was already on the ground made this small town look like it was something straight out of a Christmas movie. The rooftops were covered with fluffy white snow. The porches were strung with colored lights. And the street lamps all had big red bows.

She couldn't believe how many Christmas decorations lined the street. Every house and storefront was decked out for the season. It would take a real scrooge not to feel the holiday spirit here.

"We'll stop at the pet shop first." He slowed the pickup for the one stop light in the town. "Will you need help picking up the dog food?"

"Uh, no." She wondered what that meant. Was he planning to drop her off and keep going? But going where?

As though he could read her thoughts, he said, "I need to run to Nutz."

Surely, she hadn't heard him correctly. "You're running where?"

"To Nutz Hardware. I need to pick up some more sandpaper for the ornaments."

"Oh. Okay. Do you think the pet store will mind if I take the three musketeers with me?"

"No. Merry Kringle owns Purr 'n Woof Supplies. She loves animals. I'm sure she'd love to meet these three."

Another unique store name. She was intrigued by the unusual names. Something told her that Kringle Falls was as unique as their store names. She really wished she had more time to explore the town.

Michael pulled his pickup into the first available parking spot. It was a few spots down from the pet store. To her surprise, Michael scooped up Tank's leash. He moved swiftly, placing the pup under his arm as he exited the truck. With long strides, he rounded the front of the truck before she was able to untangle the pups from their leashes.

He opened the door for her and reached out to take Odie from her so she only had Tater Tot to manage as she stepped out of the vehicle. Not wanting the pups to get salt on their feet, she suggested they carry them to the pet shop. Michael didn't look happy as Tank licked his face, but with a pup in each arm, he set off for the pet shop.

As they made their way along the sidewalk, she noticed that most of the buildings on the street were painted in shades of red, green, and lots of white. It was all very Christmassy. This town certainly took the holiday seriously. Maybe a little too seriously.

And then she saw a white wooden sign hanging in front of the pet store. It had painted in black letters: *Purr 'n Woof Supplies*. She couldn't wait to see the interior.

She opened the door for Michael. There was the jingle of bells. When she glanced at the door, she noticed a silver jingle bell tree hanging from it. *Adorable!*

Tater Tot wiggled in her arms. "Okay. Okay." She moved farther inside and then put the pup down. "There you go. Now behave." She made sure to shorten the leash. She knew too well how excited these little guys could get. And that couldn't happen in there, because she noticed the sign just below the jingle tree that read: *You break it, you buy it*. And she was already stretching her savings as far it would go.

Michael stepped up next to her. "Everything okay?"

"Uh... Yes. I was just telling Tater to behave."

Michael nodded in understanding. "These pups definitely like to get into mischief." He glanced at Tank. "And you're the ringleader."

Tank barked as though he understood what Michael had said.

"Welcome." An older woman with short curly snow-white hair approached them. She wore gold wire-rimmed glasses. Her cheeks were rosy, and her blue eyes were attentive. "I'm Merry Kringle."

"Hi." Candi couldn't help but imagine this woman was Mrs. Claus. If the town were to put on a play, she'd most definitely fit the part. Of course, the woman's red dress and white apron helped perpetuate the idea.

The woman knelt down to fuss over the puppies. They all seemed to love her, except for Tank. He was more standoffish. He preferred to remain by Michael's side than to meet someone new.

Michael cleared his throat. "Merry, could you help Candi pick out some dog food? I need to run over to Nutz for some sandpaper and I need to get a few groceries. I won't be gone long."

"Oh, sure. No need to rush. We'll be just fine. Won't we?" She continued to pet the dogs, and in return they climbed on her in order to give her a kiss.

Candi was happy that Odie and Tater Tot were so outgoing. It'd make it so much easier to find their forever homes. However, it was Tank that concerned her. He was determined to stay with Michael, but so far Michael hadn't reciprocated those feelings.

When Michael turned to walk out the door, Tank yanked hard on the leash. Candi hadn't expected such a hard tug, and she almost lost her balance.

Tank barked and whined. It was as though the pup feared he wouldn't see Michael again.

"Tank, it's okay," she said. "He'll be back."

Tank continued to carry on.

"Why don't you let me take these two?" Merry held her hand out for Odie's and Tater Tot's leashes.

"Thank you." Candi handed over the two leashes. All the while Tank continued to yank on the leash, trying to follow Michael.

Candi scooped up Tank, who was all worked up. "It's okay, buddy. He'll be right back."

Tank wouldn't take his gaze off the door. She knew then and there that leaving this small town—leaving Michael wasn't just going to be hard for her but for Tank too. Her gaze moved to the now closed door. Too bad Michael couldn't see that he and Tank belonged together. But she wasn't giving up on convincing him of this notion.

"Is this your first visit to Kringle Falls?" Merry Kringle asked, drawing Candi's attention.

"Yes. But it isn't exactly a visit." When Merry sent her an inquisitive look, Candi explained about her accident.

"I'm so sorry to hear that. Thank goodness you and the pups are safe. So, will you be in town long?"

She shook her head. "I'm hoping to get on the road soon. I wanted to leave today but with the van in the garage and another snowstorm on the way, I've had to delay my plans."

"That's a wise suggestion. In these parts, you can never be too careful when it comes to winter storms." When Merry straightened, she asked, "What can I help you with?"

"I'm out of food for the pups. I brought just enough for the trip, not thinking we'd get stuck in the snow."

"I understand." She gestured for Candi to follow her.

They talked about the dogs, the town and the weather as they slowly picked out food for the puppies. Merry was in no hurry and for the moment, neither was Candi. She enjoyed the woman's company.

Merry had indulged the pups by giving them a couple of treats each. This totally won them over. Merry had been elevated to one of their favorite humans; well, at least that was true for Odie and Tater Tot. Tank was still looking longingly at the door, hoping Michael would walk through it.

Candi glanced around the shop, loving how it had a fenced-off training area in the back. Then she imagined Michael and Tank taking a class together. A smile pulled at the corners of her lips. They'd both be fighting to be the one in charge.

"Something amusing?" Merry arched a brow.

"Oh, it's nothing." Feeling Merry's curious gaze still on her, she said, "I was just trying to imagine Michael and Tank taking an obedience class. They are both so stubborn."

"It looks like Tank has already picked out his human," Merry said as a matter of fact.

"You noticed that?"

Merry nodded.

"The only problem is I don't think Michael got the memo."

Merry rang up the food. "You have to give Michael some time. He's been through a lot."

Candi nodded. "He told me about his family."

"It was a huge blow to the whole community. But it decimated Michael. His whole family was really concerned about him, but eventually he was able to pull himself out of that dark hole." Merry told her the total for the food.

Candi withdrew some cash from her purse and handed it over. "I can't even imagine what he went through."

"What he needs is someone to come into his life and remind him that there's more to life than his work."

If Candi didn't know better, she'd think Merry was referring to her. But that wasn't possible, because she was just passing through town.

Candi swallowed hard. "I'm sure it'll all work out when he's ready."

"Oh, I don't know. That man is really good at dragging his feet when he wants to. But I think Santa has something special in mind for him this Christmas." Merry counted out the change and handed it over.

Immediately, the thought of Michael with another woman flashed in Candi's mind. They were smiling at each other, and then they kissed. She dismissed the image, but it left behind a sour feeling in the pit of her stomach. She refused to admit what it meant because soon she was leaving Kringle Falls in her rearview mirror.

"You should consider hanging around town." Merry's voice drew her from her thoughts. "There's something magical about this place. People don't always get what they want for Christmas, but they get what they need."

Before Candi could ask what Merry's cryptic message meant, the front door jingled. She turned her head to see Michael enter the store.

Merry bagged the food. "Make sure you stop back."

"I wish I could but I won't have time. I'm already late to make it to the shelter."

"You don't always need to be in a rush. 'Tis the season to slow down and enjoy the blessings around you." Merry gave her another knowing look. "I'll be here when you need something."

"Thanks. I appreciate it." She had a feeling Merry was implying she knew something that Candi did not. She wanted to ask her about it, but Michael stepped up beside her and she lost her train of thought.

Tank rushed to Michael's side and pawed at his leg. Michael bent over to pet him. When he straightened, he asked, "Are you ready to go?"

Candi turned to him. "We are. Merry helped us find everything we needed." She turned back to the woman. "Thank you so much. You have the nicest pet store."

"You're welcome. And make sure you come back."

When they stepped outside, she noticed the snow was falling fast and collecting on the sidewalks and roadway. She had to move carefully because the sidewalks were slick, and both of her arms were around the pups. Thankfully, Tank preferred to have Michael carry him because he was the heaviest of the three pups.

Once all five of them and the dog food were situated in the pickup, Michael's phone rang. She couldn't help but feel a wee bit jealous since her phone at the moment was little more than a paper weight. She couldn't wait to get back to the house so she could charge it and be in contact with everyone.

Michael's phone conversation was quite brief. When he ended it, he said, "I'm afraid that I am needed at work."

"I thought it was your day off."

"It was until it started to snow again." They pulled out onto the now quiet road. He turned on the windshield wipers. "But don't worry. I picked up some groceries. I wasn't sure what you liked, so I just got some of the basics. Feel free to use any of it while I'm gone."

"I just feel bad that you have to go to work now after being up early because of me and the van."

"I'm good. Nothing a thermos of hot coffee and some sandwiches won't take care of."

It gave her an idea...

CHAPTER ELEVEN

H E DIDN'T WANT TO go to work.

Michael was stunned by the thought. It was the first time since he'd lost his family that he didn't want to go to work. For so long now, he'd used it as a refuge from the quietness of his house—a distraction from the constant pain in his heart.

It wasn't until Candi and those three pups suddenly appeared in his life that he realized he had been merely going through the motions of living. Every day he'd gotten out of bed in the morning, not because he was excited about the day, but rather because it was what was expected of him. He did his job, but he'd no longer let himself enjoy it.

And now he noticed that the pain in his heart was still there, but it wasn't constant. When he was around Candi, there were moments of genuine happiness. He'd forgotten how good it was to smile.

He chanced a quick glance at her. She was undeniably beautiful, but there was something else about her that drew him to her. What was it about her that had such a profound effect on him?

When they reached the house, Candi lingered outside with the pups while he rushed upstairs to get ready for another long shift at work. He knew his staff had recovered from the flu and they were fully staffed for this new storm system, but that had never kept him from work when bad weather was headed their way. And just because he had a houseguest didn't mean he should change his routine.

And to confirm his decision to head to the public works building, he got a phone call from his brother Justin. He had some questions about how best to treat the roads for this storm. The conversation took longer than he'd been expecting. By the time he made it downstairs, he found the pups stretched out in the living room—on his furniture—in front of the fireplace. He sighed but didn't bother to move them.

Tank lifted his head and looked at him as though trying to decide if it was worth his effort to get up, or if he should put his head back down on the throw pillow on the couch and go back to sleep. Michael walked over and petted his head.

"Go back to sleep." He couldn't believe how soft he was getting.

Tank let out a sigh before lowering his head.

Michael made his way toward the kitchen. He needed to pack some food for a long night of plowing. However, when he stepped into the kitchen, he came to a stop. There was Candi wrapping a sandwich in plastic wrap.

When her gaze rose to meet his, there was a rosy hue to her cheeks. "I made you some food. And..." She reached toward the counter behind her. When she turned back to him, she was holding his thermos. "And some hot coffee to keep you warm out there."

He was at a loss for words. It had been a very long time since someone had done something like this for him. Evelyn had done it a few times when they'd first married, but they had both been busy with their respective careers, so he'd fended for himself.

Candi's gesture touched him. There was a warm spot in his chest. He refused to examine what the feeling meant.

He cleared his suddenly dry throat. "I, uh... Thank you. You didn't have to do this."

She shrugged. "You didn't have to help me and the pups." The corners of her lips lifted into a smile. It made his heart beat faster. "It's just a small way to say thank you."

And then he realized he might have made a mistake by saying he'd go to work on his day off. He could have stayed there with Candi and the pups. It'd been too long since he'd had company.

There was so much he wanted to learn about Candi—like why wasn't she married? With her beauty and kindness, any guy would be crazy not to fall for her. Maybe it wasn't too late for him to change his mind. Justin was there as his backup. His little brother was more than capable of handling everything.

"You don't have to thank me," Michael said. "I'm just glad I found you." He inwardly shuddered at the thought of her and the pups being stuck in the cold with no one knowing they were there.

"I am too." She walked around the kitchen island until she was standing right in front of him. "I appreciate everything you've done for us. I'm sure you'll be relieved to have us out of here. I'm hoping they'll have the van ready to go any time now."

Her words implied that she was anxious to leave. They sucker-punched him. He lost his excitement about staying home and enjoying the latest snowstorm in front of the fireplace with her next to him.

Of course, she'd want to get going. She'd never planned to be there. She had a life to get back to in Ohio. How was he supposed to compete with that?

Whoa! Where in the world had that thought come from? He wasn't interested in her in that way.

On second thought, it was definitely best he went to work. Being snowed in with Candi had the potential to spiral out of control. He couldn't let that happen. He couldn't risk falling under her tantalizing spell.

In the next heartbeat, he realized that as much as he wanted to get back to his normal routine, he didn't want Candi to rush off into the storm. "You won't leave before the storm passes, right?"

She hesitated. It was brief, but it was long enough for him to notice. Then she nodded. "I'll wait until there's a break in the weather."

He grabbed the sandwiches and placed them into his small cooler with a couple of small ice packs. "I don't know when I'll be back."

He wanted to ask her to wait until he returned so he could see her one more time, but the words clogged in the back of his throat. It was best to say goodbye here and now. He cleared his throat. Why was saying goodbye to her so difficult?

"It was really nice meeting you," He meant it. "I hope the rest of your trip is safe."

He stuck out his hand to shake hers at the same time she reached out to him as though to hug him. They both froze. A part of him wanted to pull her close for a hug, but another part had him frozen in place.

The next thing he knew, she placed her hand in his. She gave it a squeeze that sent an electrical sensation zinging up his arm. It caused his heart to thump. Much too soon she pulled her hand away. And he was left standing there, trying to make sense of the strange sensation he'd felt when she'd touched him.

"Do you need anything else?" Her voice drew him from his scattered thoughts. When he sent her a puzzled look, she asked, "Do you need more sandwiches? Or something to go with them?"

His gaze moved to the cooler now holding the four sandwiches that she'd already made for him.

That was twice as much as he normally took with him. "That's good. Thanks again."

He hesitated for a moment. Then he forced himself to walk to the mudroom to put on his boots and coat. And then he was out the door before he said something that he would soon regret.

———*ele*———

The kitchen was clean.

The guest bed was stripped, and the sheets had been washed and were now in the dryer.

Candi had kept herself busy after Michael left. Because every time she stopped, she'd thought about their strange exchange right before he'd left for work. It was almost like he'd had something he'd wanted to say to her, but he'd hesitated. She wondered what it was, or was she just imagining things because she wasn't ready to leave Kringle Falls?

She gave herself a mental shake. She was leaving, and she wasn't coming back, so it didn't matter what she imagined he might have said. The sooner she left, the better they'd both be.

With that thought in mind, she moved to the bedroom. She gave a cursory inspection of the room to make sure she didn't forget anything. She carried her bag to the front door. Then she moved to the kitchen to gather the dogs' things. She put them all in a shopping bag.

When she placed the shopping bag next to her bag, she realized placing everything in front of the door wasn't such a good idea. She picked them up and turned in a circle, figuring where to put them so they were easily accessible and yet out of the way. She settled on putting the bags next to the armchair.

As the minutes slowly ticked by, she noticed the snow had stopped. This was a good sign. She could get back on the road. She could keep her promise to Bob to get the dogs to Maine.

She checked her phone for the umpteenth time. There was still no call from Michael about the car. She reminded herself they might not get to it right away, but that didn't keep her from hoping they would do it quickly.

As the minutes ticked by, she told herself she should call Michael to see if he heard anything. You know, just to check. Her finger hovered over the screen. After all, she needed to know what to tell Bob and the shelter in Maine when she called them.

No. She put down the phone. *They will call.*

She moved to the kitchen. She decided to make Michael something to eat for dinner. That way whenever he got home, he wouldn't have to cook himself anything.

She ended up making a shepherd's pie. Once it was in the oven, she picked up her phone once more. It was getting late. Why hadn't the garage called?

If she wanted to get on the road today, she'd have to do it soon. Maybe she'd just call. Perhaps they got too busy to call her. Yes, that was probably it. Not giving herself a chance to change her mind again, she looked up the garage's number on the internet. She dialed it.

The phone rang and rang. "Stan's Garage."

"Ah, hi. This is Candi Goodman. You have my van there. I was wondering if it was ready to go."

"Go?" The man sounded surprised. "This van isn't going anywhere for a while."

There had to be some mistake. "But it looked fine when they towed it up."

"It might have looked that way, but the undercarriage really took a beating." He went on to name more than a handful of items that needed to be replaced.

She wasn't giving up. This was too important—the puppies needed to get to Maine if they were going to find their forever homes. And if things fell through with the shelter in Maine, she didn't have a backup plan.

As she listened to the man go on about what was wrong with the van, the knot in her stomach grew tighter. She had no idea about most of what he said. She knew next to nothing about automobiles. There had never been anyone in her life to teach her. But it all sounded bad. *Very bad.*

When he paused for the briefest of moments to catch a breath, in desperation, she asked, "Could I get it fixed later? I mean, it won't die on the road... Will it?"

"No, because you won't be able to get it to the road unless you push it."

His words deflated her last bit of hope. "It's that bad?"

"Yes." His answer was bold and pointed. There was no room for her to misconstrue his answer.

"I see." She might not be able to leave right away, but that didn't mean she couldn't leave tomorrow. "How soon can you have it fixed?"

"Well, see that's the thing. We don't have all of the parts in stock. So, we have to order the others."

"Order?" She didn't like the sound of that. It meant additional time there in Kringle Falls. "How long will that take?"

"Well, with this being Thursday, the parts won't be delivered until sometime next week."

Surely she hadn't heard him correctly. "Next week? Can't you overnight the parts?"

"The problem isn't the shipping. The problem is finding parts for this old van."

"Oh." Disappointment settled over her. She had no other ideas about how to speed up this process.

"I'll let you know when the van is fixed. I would expect it to be the middle to end of next week sometime. It all depends. I know that's not what you wanted to hear. It's the best I can do."

She sighed. In other words, he had no idea when it would be repaired. "I understand." She didn't. Not really. Wasn't everything available on the internet? "Thank you for helping me."

"No problem. This is Kringle Falls, where people help each other."

After they ended the call, she tried to figure out what to do next. She should probably call the shelter.

She called the number. It rang and rang. Then it switched to a message telling her they were closed and would open the next day at 9:00 a.m.

She disconnected the call and sighed. What was she supposed to do now? Knowing she would have to tell Bob the bad news, she called him. He was happy to hear from her. He still didn't sound good, and his cough was worrisome. He told her not to worry. They'd figure everything out. The most important thing was for her to be safe. She apologized again and again. Then she told him to take care of himself, and she'd see him soon. At least she hoped so.

Ding. Ding. Ding...

The sound of the timer had her ending the call. She rushed to the kitchen and pulled the shepherd's pie out of the oven. The top was golden brown and looked perfect. She should probably be hungry, since she skipped breakfast and didn't grab much lunch, but she didn't have an appetite. She was worried—about the pups, about Bob's van, and about overstaying her welcome with Michael.

As though they sensed her mood, all three pups came over to her. They barked at her and then Odie climbed up her leg. She bent over and picked him up. She gave him a hug. He was such a sweetie.

Tank headed to the back door. He let out three loud barks. It appeared it was time to head outside.

"Come on. Let's go."

It was already dark outside. She turned off the ceiling lights in the kitchen, leaving on the pendant light over the sink. Then she slipped on her coat, hooked the leashes to the dogs, and they all headed out into the newly fallen snow. Thankfully, it wasn't nearly as much as the previous storm system.

He should have stayed home.

Michael sat in his office, feeling torn between the job he enjoyed and the beautiful woman who'd made him the sandwich he'd just finished.

The truth of the matter was that his men knew their jobs, and they were, thankfully, well-staffed. There was no need for him to come to work on his day off. He was lucky that Kringle Falls was a tourist town, and wintertime was their busiest season. It was the reason they allowed the Public Works department an ample budget to make sure they had what they needed to keep the roads in town well-maintained.

Could his department use more money to do all of the special projects that the town council thought was important? Sure. There were still places where they had to cut corners and compromise. But his staff was very good at what they did.

"Man, what are you still doing here?" Justin's voice drew Michael from his thoughts.

He glanced up at his youngest brother. "Where would you like me to be?"

"At home with your guest."

Michael's heart launched into his throat. He hadn't mentioned Candi to anyone. He hadn't expected word to get out so quickly. Then again, Kringle Falls was a small town with a busy rumor mill.

"She doesn't need me hanging around." He wasn't about to let on that he enjoyed her company. "Besides, she's leaving as soon as she gets her van back."

"Maybe you can convince her to stick around a little longer." Justin waggled his brows.

Michael sighed. "Now why would I do that?" As soon as the words crossed his lips, he knew he'd made a mistake. He rushed on to say, "I barely know her. Besides, she has to get on with her life."

"Maybe you should get on with your life too."

"What's that supposed to mean?"

Justin propped himself against the door jamb and crossed his arms. "It means you don't have a life. Sure, you go through the motions. You get up in the morning, go to work, and go home. That's it."

Michael rubbed the back of his neck. He didn't want to have this conversation. It was way too similar to the one he had with his mother when she got on his case for not putting himself out there and dating again. He had no interest in getting involved with anyone. Suddenly, Candi's image came to mind. If he was going to date anyone, it would be her. She was tempting, but it wasn't going to happen for a number of reasons.

"There's nothing wrong with my life."

Justin rolled his eyes. "Tell me that you don't believe that."

Michael stood. "I don't have time for this discussion."

"Because you need to go home. The snow has stopped, and there's nothing here that needs your attention."

Michael smothered a sigh. Then he decided to turn this conversation around. "Are you trying to get rid of me so you can be in charge?"

Justin's eyes momentarily widened as anger flickered in them. A moment later, he shook his head. "I see what you did there. You're trying to deflect. Well, if it makes you feel better, then yes, I want to be in charge. Now, will you go home?"

The thought of seeing Candi before she left was very tempting. And technically, this was his day off. The storm was winding down early, and there wasn't any reason he couldn't go home.

"Fine. I have a couple of emails to answer, and then I'm out of here." He didn't miss the shocked look on Justin's face.

"Okay then. Good for you." Justin smiled like he'd just won an argument or something.

"Don't look at me like that. I planned to go home before you said anything."

"Uh-huh." Justin nodded as he smiled at him like a Cheshire cat.

"Don't you have some work to do?"

Justin turned and whistled as he walked away.

Michael shook his head again as he sat down at the desk and tried to remember the email he was planning to write.

Chapter Twelve

H E WONDERED WHAT SHE had been up to.

Michael let himself into the house. He glanced from the mudroom into the kitchen, but Candi wasn't there. He also expected to be greeted by three boisterous dogs. And yet all he was met with was silence.

He stood there for a moment. He should be happy for the peace and quiet. And yet there was a part of him that worried Candi might have left already.

After he hung up his coat and slipped off his work boots, he walked to the guest room. The door was open. He glanced inside. It was dark, but there was enough moonlight coming through the window to see that the bed was empty.

She's really gone.

He flipped on the light switch and stepped into the room. The bed was neatly made, and her suitcase was gone. There were no dog leashes on the chest of drawers. There was absolutely no sign that Candi had ever been there. It was like she'd been a figment of his imagination.

He reached for his phone, anxious to hear her voice. His finger hesitated over the screen. What would he say to her? That he wanted to hear her voice? *No.* That he missed her? *Definitely not.*

He returned his phone to his back pocket and made his way to the kitchen. He noticed that she'd left a light on for him. And there was something else...

He inhaled deeper. *Mm...* He sniffed his way over to the stove, where he found a casserole dish covered with aluminum foil. He touched the dish and found it was slightly warm. So, she hadn't been gone that long.

Was it possible she waited around as long as she could in hopes of seeing him again? The thought warmed a spot in his chest. Maybe he would call her and thank her for... *Hm...* He should probably look to see what she'd cooked him before he spoke to her.

He moved to the sink to wash up, but as he reached to turn on the water, he noticed a light in the workshop. That was strange. He hadn't noticed it on his way into the house, but then again, he'd been utterly distracted with thoughts of Candi.

He never left the lights on. Was it possible someone had broken in? But this was Kringle Falls, where there was rarely any crime. It was why he used to tease Parker that being the sheriff meant he had the easiest job in town. His brother didn't think it was funny.

However, there was always a first. He moved to the mudroom. He looked around for something to defend himself with. *Broom? No. Snow shovel? Maybe.* And then his gaze landed on the baseball bat in the corner. It had been there since his last softball game in the autumn.

He slipped on his boots, grabbed the bat, and headed out the back door. The freshly fallen snow cushioned his steps, allowing him to make a silent approach.

He stopped at the side door. He didn't hear any noise inside. He placed his hand on the doorknob and slowly turned it.

He eased the door open. He didn't see anyone. He stepped inside, and that was when he spotted Candi sitting at the work table. She was painting an ornament.

When she glanced up, she jumped. She pressed a hand to her chest. "I didn't hear you come in." Then her gaze drifted down to the bat in his hands. Her brows drew together. "What are you doing with that?"

He set the bat aside. "I...uh, saw it in the mudroom and realized I had forgotten to put it away." It at least sounded plausible, though the furrow in her brow let him know she wasn't fully buying his story. Perhaps it was time to change the subject. "What are you working on?"

"I thought I'd paint some more of the ornaments." She held up the reindeer she was working on.

"That looks really nice." She put his painting to shame.

She turned the ornament around so she could look at it. "Do you really think so?"

He nodded. "I do. You're talented."

"I used to paint a lot when I was younger, but then I got so busy with college and then teaching that I didn't make time for my hobbies." Her gaze lifted to meet his. "But you gave it back to me. Thank you."

When she smiled at him, he felt the warmth of her smile deep in his chest. His heart thumped. He didn't know how long they stared into each other's eyes before he gathered himself and glanced away.

He swallowed hard. "I'm glad you remembered how much you enjoy painting, but I didn't really have much to do with it. That was all you."

"Oh, quit being modest. I'm really enjoying myself."

It was only then that Tank stood up and barked. He ran around the table and headed straight for Michael.

Tank jumped up, putting his paws on Michael's pant leg. He barked until he picked up the pup. At the rate Tank was growing, he wouldn't be able to pick him up much longer.

Michael ran his hand over the pup's head. "You look like you're still half asleep."

"I let them play in the snow for a while. It wore them out. They've been sleeping near the wood stove."

He glanced up to find the other two pups sitting in front of him, waiting for him to fuss over them too. He knelt down and was immediately jumped on by the pups.

"I talked to the garage about the van." She hesitated.

"I was wondering why I hadn't heard from them. What did they say?"

"Well... The van has a lot of damage to it."

"I'm sorry." And he was, but he also felt relieved that she wouldn't be leaving quite so soon. "But it's not surprising, since that was quite a ride you all took down over that embankment."

"I was hoping they would be able to fix it in a day or two, but they're having problems finding the right parts. They said since it's an older van, the parts are harder to come by. And I know that we've overstayed our welcome, so if you could give us a ride into town, I can get a room at a motel or something."

"I'm afraid that won't work." When she sent him a questioning look, he continued. "They aren't going to let you stay there with three puppies."

She sighed. "I had a feeling you were going to say something like that."

"So, I guess you all will have to stay here."

She frowned. "But I feel horrible about disrupting your life."

Under his breath he muttered, "Some people don't think I have a life."

"What did you say?"

He shook his head. "You don't have to worry about staying here."

"Can I pay you?"

"No. Absolutely not."

"But there has to be some way I can pay you back."

He stopped to give it some thought. "Well, you could keep cooking for me."

"It's a deal."

He shook his head. "I wasn't serious. You don't have to cook. I can take care of myself."

"I'm sure you can, but it's the least I can do."

"But you're also painting the ornaments for me, and from the look of the house, you've done some cleaning."

"I hope you don't mind. I had some time on my hands."

"Who am I to complain about having a spiffed-up house? But right now, I'm starved. Would you like to join me for a late dinner?"

"I thought you'd never ask." She carried her paint brushes to the sink and rinsed them off.

When she smiled at him, his pulse raced. There was something special about her—something that made him want to spend more time at home—to forget about his promise to himself that he wouldn't love again—that he wouldn't risk his scarred heart.

—ele—

Dinner was finished.

The kitchen was cleaned up.

Candi looked over at Michael, but before she could say what was on her mind, a yawn escaped her lips. Maybe it was best to leave the conversation until the morning.

As she studied his face while he read something on his phone, she could see his exhaustion. But there was something else beneath the tiredness. It took her a moment and then she realized what it was—sadness.

She didn't have to guess to know what had put it there—the loss of his family. Her thoughts turned to the pillow cover that was folded up in her purse. She felt awful that the pups had destroyed it.

Michael lowered his phone and looked at her. "I should let you get some rest. Thank you for dinner. It was delicious."

"You're welcome. Good night." She turned toward the guest room.

She expected the pups to follow her, but when she looked down, she realized she only had two of them with her. Tank was missing. Why wasn't she surprised? That dog had taken an instant liking to Michael, not that she could blame him. There was a lot to like about him.

She felt bad for Michael. He was obviously still mourning his family. It explained why there wasn't one single Christmas decoration in the house.

She wanted to give him a bit of holiday spirit, but she had no idea how to do that. She'd have to give it some more thought.

Once in her room, she looked at the pups and told them to stay. She exited the room, closing the door behind her. She didn't see him in the living room. She called Tank's name. On her way to the kitchen, she paused at the bottom of the steps.

"Michael!"

"Yeah." He moved to stand at the top of the steps. "What do you need?"

"Is Tank up there?"

His brows scrunched together. "I don't think so. Let me look."

He walked away. She could hear him calling out to the pup. And then he returned to the steps.

"He's up here. He's in my bed under the covers."

She couldn't stop the smile that crossed her face. Tank had a mind of his own. He could be as stubborn as the man in front of her.

"Stop smiling," Michael said. "This isn't funny. He can't get used to this because sooner or later he's going to his forever home."

She wasn't sure if he was saying this for her sake or for his own. Was it possible that Michael's crusty exterior was cracking a bit? Had Tank gotten to him? She didn't think it would be hard, considering that ball of fluff was nothing but a snuggle bug.

Gathering herself, she subdued the smile, but it took effort. "Would you like me to get him?"

Michael hesitated, as though it took him effort to figure out the answer. "You might as well just leave him because we both know that he'll escape your room sometime during the night, and he'll be back up here."

The tug at the corners of her mouth grew with intensity. "Are you sure?"

Michael nodded. "Night."

"Good night."

She couldn't turn away soon enough, because she finally lost the fight, and a great big grin pulled at her lips. She had a feeling Tank had found his forever home.

CHAPTER THIRTEEN

SNOWFLAKES FLUTTERED TO THE ground.

The next morning, Candi stared out the window at the flurries. She didn't know what to do with herself. She wasn't used to sitting around with nothing to do. And with Christmas a couple of weeks away, there were so many things to do before the big day.

Since she didn't have much money, she liked to make gifts for her friends. However, when she lost her job, she'd kept herself busy by knitting scarves for everyone. She only had one to finish. Luckily, it wouldn't take her long to complete it, once she got home.

She checked the time. When it was finally 9:00 a.m., she called the shelter in Maine. The phone rang and rang before it switched to the answering machine. She left a brief message and her phone number. She hoped they would call her right back. By now they must think she wasn't coming, when that couldn't be further from the truth.

Odie barked at her and then ran to the back door. It was time to go out into the cold. She called for the other two. She wasn't going outside more than once. With their leashes on, they headed out.

While they took care of business, she crouched down and scooped up some snow. She pressed it into a ball between her gloved hands. She noticed how well it held together. This was perfect snow to make a snowman.

Memories started flooding her mind of how her mother would help her make a snowman each winter. Her mother had as much fun doing it as Candi did. They were good memories that filled her heart with love. She wondered if Michael had similar memories. She hoped so.

After the pups were back inside, she got an idea. She moved to the front yard where there was a lot of undisturbed snow.

She pulled out her phone and turned on some Christmas music. Since no one lived close by, she turned up the volume. She sang along as she made a great big snowball. She rolled it into position and then started on the second snowball. She had to be careful with this one because if she made it too big, she wouldn't be able to lift it by herself.

After testing the weight every now and then, she finally had to stop. It took all of her might to lift the snowball into position.

Now there was only one more to go. It didn't take her nearly as long to make the head. She positioned it on top and then picked up some extra snow to reinforce the neck.

She stepped back and looked at her creation. She couldn't help but think her mother would be proud of her effort.

But she wasn't finished. This was the hard part. She needed eyes, a nose, and mouth. Not to mention some clothing. *Hm...*

She rushed back inside. It was only then she noticed how cold she'd gotten. She made a cup of coffee to warm herself up.

While she defrosted, she checked her phone to make sure she hadn't missed any calls. Though, she didn't see how that would be possible since she'd been playing music on it. A call would have interrupted the carols. Still, she looked. As she suspected, there were no missed calls.

As though by sheer willpower, the phone rang. When she looked at the caller ID, she found it wasn't the shelter. It was Michael.

She pressed the phone to her ear. "Hey, aren't you supposed to be working?"

"Well, hello to you too." There was a smile in his voice. "I just wanted to check in. Is there anything you need?"

Immediately, the items she needed for the snowman came to mind, but she dismissed them. She would make due with whatever she could find.

"Not that I can think of. Are you coming home soon?" She didn't miss how domesticated this conversation sounded, but she refused to admit to herself that it meant anything. Michael was just being nice.

"Do you need me to?"

"No." She stopped herself from admitting she was bored without him around.

"Oh." Was that a note of disappointment in his voice? Or was she just imagining things?

An awkward silence ensued. She wondered if he'd been expecting a different answer.

Deciding it was best to change the subject, she asked, "Is there anything special you'd like for dinner?"

"I was thinking we'd go into town for dinner. What do you think?"

Considering she wanted to see more of Kringle Falls, she loved the idea. "I think it's a great idea."

"Good. I'll see you later."

"See you then." As she disconnected the call, she worried her bottom lip.

What was she going to wear to dinner? She had no idea where he was taking her. Maybe she should have asked a few questions. But it was too late now. She wasn't calling him back. She didn't want to make a big deal out of this date.

There was a distinct hiss as she sucked in air. She halted her thoughts. Why in the world did she refer to their dinner as a date? He hadn't asked her out. Well, he had, but there had been absolutely no romantic intention behind it. Right? She couldn't let herself think that his invitation was anything more than it was—a friendly gesture.

To keep herself from dwelling on the dinner invitation, she chugged what was left of her coffee, and then she went in search of items for the snowman.

First, she headed to her bedroom. She rummaged through her suitcase and came up with a red knitted scarf. A friend made it for her a few years ago. She smiled as she ran her fingers over the soft yarn. But the scarf was all she came up with.

She headed to the kitchen and found a carrot. But he still needed eyes and a mouth. She already knew she had no chance of finding a top hat. But she'd make do with what she was able to find.

She checked on the pups, who were all asleep in the living room. It looked like daycare central with those furbabies sprawled about.

Now she needed to figure out something for the snowman's eyes. She turned in a circle, hoping something would come to mind. Perhaps she'd have better luck out in the workshop. The more she thought about it, the more she liked the idea. She slipped on her boots and coat.

In the workshop, she flipped on all of the lights. Surely there would be something out here she could use. It had to be something that Michael wouldn't miss.

She moved to the garbage can. It was filled with scraps of wood. It was then that she got an idea.

She pulled out bits of wood and put them on the workbench. She reached for his cordless rotary tool. She attached the saw attachment, and then she set to work cutting little squares. They ended up all different sizes but for her purposes, it didn't matter.

She grabbed a paint brush and the black paint. In no time she had fake coal. Luckily the paint was fast-drying. They'd be ready in no time.

After checking on the pups again, she moved on to the snowman. She stood back and inspected it. She decided it needed a little more snow here and there. Then she added the carrot nose and wrapped the scarf around the snowman's neck. She broke a couple of twigs from a nearby tree and used them for the arms.

She rushed back to the workshop. She not only grabbed her faux chunks of coal, but she spotted an old broom. She rushed back outside.

A few minutes later, the snowman was complete. And he wasn't too bad if she did say so herself. She reached for her phone to take a picture, but before she could press the app, the phone rang.

She was relieved when she saw it was the shelter calling her back. She pressed the phone to her ear. "Hello."

"Ms. Goodman, this is Betty Graham. I just got your message. I'm sorry to hear about your accident. Are you all right?"

"I am. And so are the puppies. But the van didn't fare as well. It's in the garage being repaired, and that's why I won't be able to make it to the shelter until the end of the week." She refused to acknowledge that it could be longer.

"I'm really sorry about your troubles, but I'm not going to be able to take the puppies."

"But..."

"My husband surprised me with plans for a holiday cruise. The shelter is almost empty."

This couldn't be happening. Desperate, Candi asked, "What if I was able to get the puppies to you tomorrow?"

"I'm afraid that still wouldn't leave me enough time to find them a proper home. I hope you're able to make other arrangements."

Candi wasn't sure what to say. She knew this was her fault. If she hadn't gotten lost and wrecked, the pups would have been there, and hopefully, found their forever homes.

"Oops. That's my other line. I have to go. Merry Christmas."

"Merry Christmas." Candi ended the call.

She forgot about taking the photo of the snowman. She went inside and took off her coat and boots.

She sank down on the couch. Tears stung the backs of her eyes. Nothing was working out and it was her fault.

The pups got up and gathered around her. It was like they knew there was something wrong. Tater Tot licked her cheek.

She ran her hand over each of them. They were each so sweet and loving. They deserved to have their forever home. And it was her fault that hadn't happened.

Her vision blurred with tears. How had she let this happen? She'd had a simple job—she had to drive to Maine. That was it. And she'd failed.

He couldn't wait to get home.

Michael couldn't remember the last time he'd been anxious to go home. For so long, he'd thought he'd never be happy again, but he was happy. Candi had given him back so much.

He was tempted to call Stan's Garage and bribe them to take even longer repairing the van. It wasn't like he would really do something like that, but the fact the thought had crossed his mind told him a lot.

He wheeled his pickup into the driveaway. His attention was immediately drawn to the snowman in his front yard. *What in the world?* He let out a laugh. It was cute and goofy all at the same time. Candi was forever surprising him.

He turned off the engine. He was glad he'd asked her to dinner. It just seemed like the right thing to do after she'd turned his house back into a home—a warm, comforting place.

He moved to the side door. He let himself into the mudroom and was quickly greeted by Tank followed by Odie and Tater Tot.

"Candi?"

"In here."

He kicked off his boots and hung up his coat before heading to the living room. He found her sitting on the couch without the television on. He sat down in the armchair at the end of the couch.

When he looked at her, he noticed her splotchy complexion and bloodshot eyes. His chest tightened with worry. "What's wrong?"

She glanced away. "It's nothing for you to worry about."

His voice softened. "Candi, talk to me. Maybe I can help."

She hesitated so long he didn't think she was going to open up to him. But then she said in a soft voice—so soft that he had to strain to hear her, "I took too long. The shelter won't take the puppies now, and I can't keep them. My lease forbids pets."

He felt bad for her. "What about the shelter where you got them?"

"The building has been sold. The shelter no longer exists."

He knew this was the place where he should offer to take them, but he couldn't do that. His work had him away from home for long periods of time. And there was the part where he wasn't ready to open his heart. He had built such a tall and deep wall around it that he didn't even know if it was possible to tear it down.

There had to be a better solution. He gave it some thought and then something came to him. He didn't know if it was a sure thing, so he didn't want to say anything until he had something concrete.

He got to his feet. "I need to make a call."

Candi didn't say anything as he made his way upstairs and entered his bedroom. With the door closed, he placed the phone call.

CHAPTER FOURTEEN

ALL FIVE OF THEM climbed into the pickup.

As the snowy scenery passed by outside the window, Candi wondered what Michael was up to. After he'd returned from making his mysterious call, all he'd said was to get ready and that they were taking a ride—all five of them.

When she asked questions, all he'd tell her was that she'd have to wait and see. The fact that he'd insisted they bring the pups had her thinking it might have something to do with them. But there was no way he'd found homes for them so quickly. So, if it wasn't that, what else could it be?

She didn't have to wonder for long, because it was a short drive into town. She was disappointed they didn't have to take the bridge over the river so she could see Kringle Falls again.

Instead, she was treated to an entire town that was decorated for Christmas. The decorations were everywhere. She'd never seen a town that made such an effort to decorate. It must take them a long time to do all of this.

"When do they start decorating?" she asked.

"You mean the town?"

"Yes. It's very impressive." She pulled her phone out of her purse so she could take some photos. She wanted to show Bob and Stacy when she got home.

"You don't know anything about Kringle Falls, do you?"

She felt like she should know more than she did. "No."

Michael was quiet for a moment, as though deciding where he should start his explanation. "Kringle Falls is a Christmas town."

"I can see that."

He shook his head. "That's not what I'm saying. This town celebrates Christmas year-round."

Her mouth gaped. "Really? Wow. That's a lot of Christmas."

He nodded. "It's been that way my entire life. In fact, I don't know when it started. But people travel here from all over to visit. There's the Santa museum, Elf Playhouse, and so much more. It's a great town if you're into that kind of stuff."

She studied him for a moment. "You make it sound like you aren't."

He shrugged. "My wife used to work at the Elf Playhouse. She used to say that Kringles carried Christmas in their hearts year-round, so why not let it show."

Candi smiled. "Your wife sounds like she was a really positive person."

"She was..." His voice drifted away, as though he were getting caught up in his memories of her.

"Evelyn was quiet. She had a big heart, but she was an introvert."

She liked that he was comfortable enough around her to speak about them. His voice became animated the more he spoke of Evelyn and Noah. Her heart broke for him that he'd lost them far too soon.

Michael pulled the truck into a parking spot on the side of the road. She glanced around and recognized where they were. This was close to the pet shop. Was that their destination?

Michael took Tank and Odie. She only had to manage Tater Tot as she stepped out of the truck. Thankfully, the sidewalks had been cleared. Still, worried there would be salt on them, she held on to Tater Tot.

She couldn't hold back her curiosity any longer. "What are we doing here?"

Michael sent her an I-know-but-you-don't smile. However, he came to a stop in front of the pet shop. She opened the door with her free hand and let him pass by her. She then followed him inside.

Merry Kringle came rushing to the front of the store. "I thought I heard someone come in." She sent them both a warm smile. "And look at those cuties you have with you." She proceeded to pet each of them.

Michael turned to Candi. "I brought you here because Merry has been gracious enough to help the pups find their forever home."

"That's wonderful," Candi said. It didn't feel wonderful. She knew this moment was coming, but she'd refused to think about having to say goodbye to these three musketeers.

Her gaze lingered on each of them. How was she supposed to say goodbye to them? She loved each of them.

But in the next breath, she realized she couldn't keep them. And as much as she loved them, they would find homes filled with love. She just didn't know this was going to hurt so much.

"Isn't that right?" Michael's gaze met hers.

Oops. She had no idea what had been said because her mind had wondered.

Heat rushed to her face. "Sorry. What did you say?"

Michael's brows arched. "We were talking about how good-natured the dogs are, even if they can get into mischief if left alone for too long."

"Oh, yes. That's true. Although, I think Tank is the ringleader when it comes to making trouble."

Michael looked at Tank, who was sitting on the floor next to him. "Are you the chief troublemaker?"

"Bark. Bark."

They all let out a laugh. Tank looked proud of his new title.

Candi hugged Tater Tot before placing him on the floor. Merry held out her hand for the leash. This was all happening so quickly.

There was an ache in her heart as she surrendered the leash to the kind woman. When she'd volunteered for this job, she never imagined all they'd go through together or how sweet they were to snuggle with at night. Boy, was she going to miss them.

And then everyone turned to Michael. He immediately handed Merry the leashes for Tank and Odie.

When she knelt down to pet the dogs, Michael said, "I'll meet you in the pickup."

She turned her head to see him walk away. She couldn't believe he'd turned his back so easily on Tank. The husky was pulling on his leash and frantically barking at Michael to come back.

She tried to soothe Tank as she reached out to pet him. "I'm sorry, boy. You're going to be okay. It's all going to work out."

Tank kept fussing. It broke her heart. How could Michael just walk away? She'd witnessed how those two had bonded.

"Tank isn't going to be happy about the separation."

"He is Michael's shadow. He isn't going to understand what's going on."

"Maybe Michael just needs some time. I'm glad he has you to help him step out of the shadows and back into the land of the living."

"Oh, no." Candi shook her head. "I'm not his friend. Well, I am, but what I mean is that I'm, uh, leaving soon." Heat swirled in her chest and rushed up to her cheeks.

Merry sent her a warm smile that eased her discomfort. "No one ever knows the future. After all, you didn't expect to end up in Kringle Falls, did you?" When Candi shook her head, Merry said,

"Maybe you were meant to be here. After all, Christmas is a magical season." The woman's blue eyes twinkled as she smiled at her.

Candi couldn't explain it, but she got the distinct feeling everything was going to work out. But how could that be? So far, her trip had been a disaster. Yet there was a calmness about her and an assured feeling that it was all going to work out.

With the greatest regret, she said one last goodbye to the pups and thanked Merry before making her way to the pickup. Michael had the motor running and warm air blowing out of the vents to take the chill out of the air. However, there was still one thing bothering her. She thought for sure Michael would have kept Tank.

She glanced over at him at the same time that he looked at her. Why wouldn't he keep Tank? Was he that broken on the inside that he couldn't let himself care for a puppy?

"Don't look at me that way." Michael's voice was stern.

She didn't say anything, but she didn't turn away either. She'd finally figured out that he used his grouchy exterior as a shield—to keep people at a distance. But now she knew the truth. He was nothing more than a marshmallow on the inside—all sweet and soft.

He shook his head as he turned away. "It's not like you kept any of them either."

That was true and it dug at her heart. But she wasn't abandoning them either. She truly believed they'd find their forever homes. But if that didn't happen, she'd take them back. She didn't have a plan for where they'd live, but she'd figure something out. They hadn't come this far together just for her to bail on the pups now.

He glanced at her with a smug look like he'd won the argument, she countered. "There's a difference. I can't keep the pups, because my lease doesn't allow it. But there's nothing keeping you from giving Tank a home. That dog is utterly devoted to you. He looks at you with such adoration."

"Stop. Just stop." Michael focused on his mirrors as he pulled out into traffic.

Part of her wanted to keep pushing him until he turned the truck around and went back to the pet shop to get Tank, but she didn't. She knew by the tone of his voice that there was a war waging inside of him. The question was what part of him would win?

Instead of heading back to the house, he pulled into a little restaurant called the Kringle Diner. At first, she was confused. Then she remembered that he'd promised to take her to dinner.

The problem was that she didn't have an appetite after the agonizing scene where she had to say goodbye to the pups. And yet she felt this was important to Michael. From everything she'd learned about him, it seemed he didn't get out much. Maybe if she and Tank were lucky, this dinner would put another crack in Michael's crusty exterior.

With that thought in mind, she got out of the truck and joined him on the sidewalk. She walked up to the front of the Kringle Diner. Michael opened the door for her.

She thanked him and then stepped inside. She wished she'd taken more time with her appearance before they'd left the house. But it was too late to worry about that now.

What had he done?

Michael couldn't stop thinking about the sad look in Tank's eyes. The memory stabbed at his scarred heart.

As much as he wanted to turn around and go back for Tank, he wouldn't allow himself. He couldn't open his heart up. He couldn't put himself at risk of loving and losing again.

He pushed the troubling thoughts to the back of his mind. The problem was that they wouldn't stay there. Thoughts of Tank kept crystallizing in the forefront of his mind. He could still hear the dog's anguished barks.

Maybe some conversation would help distract him. "This is the oldest restaurant in town."

Candi glanced around. "It's cute."

He looked around, trying to see it like she would. The walls were white with red trim. The tables all had red linoleum tabletops. There was a skinny Christmas tree in the corner. Coming here was like having Christmas dinner with a bunch of friends because everyone in Kringle Falls knew each other. It was what happened in a town of twelve hundred give or take a few.

No sooner had they been seated and their menus in hand than he heard a familiar voice. "Michael, what are you doing here?"

He looked up to see his parents headed in his direction. It was too late to duck out of sight. He didn't want his mother to make a big deal about him being there with Candi.

When they stopped next to the table, he said, "Hey, Mom. Pops."

His mother beamed as she looked at the two of them. He wished she would stop that. She didn't have to say a word for him to know she was jumping to all of the wrong conclusions.

"Hi," his mother said. "I'm Tricia Bishop and this is my husband, John." She held out her hand.

Candi placed her hand in his mother's. As they shook, she said, "It's nice to meet you both. I'm Candi Goodman."

His mother looked at him. "I didn't know you were seeing anyone."

He inwardly groaned. "That's because I'm not." When his mother's gaze darted to Candi and then back at him, as though pointing out the error of his statement, he said, "We're just friends."

"I see."

Michael looked at his father, hoping he would help him. Michael loved his mother, but when she thought someone needed help, she could be meddlesome. It appeared she thought he needed help with his love life when nothing could be further from the truth. He didn't have a love life—not anymore.

He wondered if this was what Evelyn would have wanted for him—eternal and complete devotion. It wasn't like they ever talked about things like that. They'd been young. They never thought the end would come so suddenly—so traumatically.

Evelyn used to say that you only got this one life to live, so live it to your fullest. He wondered if she'd feel the same way when it came to him introducing another woman into his life. As Candi and his mother spoke, he couldn't help but wonder if Candi could be that person.

He didn't have a chance to come to terms with that startling thought when his mother said, "I expect to see you both for Sunday dinner."

And then his parents walked away before he could tell her that wasn't going to happen. She knew he rarely went to Sunday dinner since Evelyn and Noah passed. He always had an excuse. Most of the time, it had something to do with his work. Was it wrong of him to hope the winter storm would stretch out through the weekend?

"Why are you frowning?" Candi's voice drew him from his thoughts.

"I'm sorry about my mother. We don't have to go."

"But I'd like to. You know, meet the rest of your family. How many brothers did you say you had?"

"Three. The oldest is Parker. He's the town's sheriff. Then there's Colin. He's a veterinarian here in town. And then there's Justin. He works with me, doing township maintenance."

"I can't even imagine what it must have been like growing up with three siblings. It must have been so much fun."

He wasn't in a good mood between leaving Tank at the pet store and then his mother insisting they go to dinner that weekend. Taking Candi to his parents' house would feel like—like he was bringing home his girlfriend to meet his family. And this was not that case. Not even close.

When he noticed Candi was looking at him with an expectant look on her face, he cleared his throat. "The truth is that the good times definitely outweighed any of the bad stuff. I wouldn't be the man I am today without my brothers and the lessons we learned together. And trust me, there were a lot of them."

"I bet. I can't even imagine how your parents kept up with all of you."

He smiled and nodded. "My father would tell you that we were responsible for every one of the gray hairs on his head."

Candi laughed. The warm sound eased the band of stress that was wrapped around his chest. By the time the waitress made it to their table, they both ended up ordering club sandwiches with a side of fries and ketchup.

He liked that they had that in common, in addition to loving dogs. He wondered what else they had in common. And so, they kept talking throughout their meal, and they'd even opted to get dessert—a slice of pie. He chose cherry. She picked pumpkin. Okay, so they couldn't have everything in common. That would be boring.

CHAPTER FIFTEEN

I T HADN'T BEEN A date.

Still, it had been a very nice evening.

Saturday morning without the pups around, Candi didn't know what to do with herself. She kept thinking she heard the pups or that she should go check on them. She missed them so much. She wondered if they missed her too. She hoped not, because she wanted them to be happy.

She wanted to go visit them, to see how they were doing. She forgot to tell Merry that Odie didn't eat all of his food at once and that you had to watch or Tater Tot would eat his own food as well as Odie's, which would make him sick. And if you didn't keep after Tank, he would play too rough for the smaller dogs. There were just so many things she wanted to tell Merry.

But without her own vehicle, she was stuck. Of course, she could ask Michael to borrow his pickup, but knowing him, he'd insist on driving her. He'd already done so much for her that she didn't want him going out of his way for her again.

Michael quietly entered the living room and caught her sitting on the couch, staring off into space. He was wearing a pair of dark jeans and a red and gray flannel shirt. She'd never cared for flannel until she saw it on him. It suited him.

"Do you want an early lunch?" he asked.

She shook her head. "No thanks."

"But you must be hungry. You didn't eat any breakfast."

"I'm not hungry." She held up her coffee mug. "This is all I need."

He frowned at her. "How about we get out of here?"

Her heart leapt. "You mean to see the puppies?"

He visibly swallowed. "I was actually thinking about going for a snowmobile ride."

"Oh." She tried and failed to keep the disappointment from her voice. "It's okay. You go ahead."

He shifted his weight from one foot to the other as the silence between them ensued. "What if we compromise?"

She lifted her gaze to meet his. "What do you have in mind?"

"What if we ride the snowmobile into town?"

She shrugged.

"I wasn't finished," he said. "And while we're in town, we could check on the pups."

Her gaze met his. "Really? I mean, I don't want you to go out of your way for me."

"I wouldn't mind seeing them either."

She knew it. He missed Tank.

She got to her feet before he could change his mind. "Let's go."

"You can't go like that."

She glanced down at her red and white snowflake sweater and her faded blue jeans. "I don't have anything else to wear."

"But I do. Wait a minute." He disappeared up the steps. A few minutes later, he returned with a black snow suit and a black helmet. "I think these will fit you. Evelyn was close to your size."

She wasn't sure how she felt about wearing his dead wife's things. Still, she didn't miss the significance of this moment. He was starting to let down his guard. His past and present were beginning to merge. Maybe there was hope for him after all.

He put a pair of snow boots in front of her. "I don't know if these will fit or not. But I thought you might want to wear them so you don't mess up your white ones."

She looked down at the black snow boots. Sure. Why not?

"Thank you." She took the bib overalls and jacket. "They look like they should fit."

"Good." He sent her a reassuring smile. "I'll just go grab my things in the mudroom."

She put on the things and found them to be a little big on her, but that was better than being too small. She carried the boots to the mudroom and slipped them on.

Michael zipped his jacket and turned to her. He was quiet for a moment, and she wondered if he was truly seeing her or if he was caught up in memories of his wife. Either way, it was okay. His wife and son would always be a part of him. To care about him, she had to accept that fact.

Her heart skipped a beat. Did she care about him? The thought swirled round and round in her mind.

"Are you okay?" Michael's voice drew her from her shock.

"Um, yes. Thank you for letting me wear these. They fit."

He sent her a small smile. "Glad to hear it."

Since this was her first experience on a snowmobile, Michael gave her a brief rundown of how everything worked. To her relief, she didn't have to remember half of what he'd told her, because she'd be riding in back and holding on to him. He took it slow in the beginning, but as she got used to the feel of the snowmobile, he picked up the speed. She had no idea what fun she'd been missing. Buying a snowmobile was now on her wish list. Of course, she was going to have to find a job first, and then there was the part about living in an apartment. It might make it a little difficult to store a snowmobile. But she let go of the questions without answers, and instead, hung onto Michael and enjoyed the sensation of having the snowmobile glide over the snow.

But there was another sensation that was even better—being this close to Michael. Her heart pitter-pattered in her chest. She could definitely get used to this.

Eventually, they ended up on the edge of town. He parked the snowmobile and got off. "Don't worry. It's not far from here."

Side-by-side, they walked toward the pet store. The sunshine had drawn out people that had spent the past few days in their houses because of the weather.

Most everyone said hello as they passed by. Candi noticed the surprised looks on some of the passersby's faces upon seeing her with Michael. Some tried to hide their shock. Others weren't so subtle and openly stared.

If Michael noticed, he didn't say anything. She hoped her presence in his life wouldn't cause him any problems. That was the very last thing she wanted for him after the kindness he'd shown her.

When they arrived at the pet store, she wasn't sure what she was expecting when she entered the shop, but it wasn't the silence. She started to worry that the puppies weren't there.

But as they made their way toward the back of the shop, she found the three musketeers in a playpen. As soon as they spotted them, excited barks abounded.

Merry stepped out of what appeared to be her office. When she spotted them, she smiled. "Hello."

"I hope you don't mind," Candi said. "We wanted to stop by and check on the puppies."

"I don't mind at all. They are excited to see you too."

Michael didn't wait for an invitation, he let himself into the playpen. He sat down on a stool, and the pups climbed all over him.

When he smiled, it eased the stress on his face and made him look ten years younger. Happiness definitely looked good on him. She had hoped that by seeing Tank again, Michael would come to his senses and take Tank home where he belonged. Well, maybe not this exact moment, considering they'd rode the snowmobile. But it wouldn't be that hard to go back to the house and get the pickup.

She joined him in the playpen. The puppies lathered her with love. She'd missed them so much.

Before they left, she remembered to tell Merry about the puppies' habits, both good and bad. Merry paid attention. And then told her not to worry. They would be all right.

As Tank played tug-of-war with Michael, Candi gestured for Merry to step to the side with her. She whispered, "Can you hold off on finding a home for Tank?"

"Because he already has a home?" When Candi nodded, Merry said, "I take it Michael still hasn't changed his mind?"

Candi shook her head. "I don't understand it. Tank loves him. And Michael loves him right back. But he won't admit it to me or himself."

"Sometimes when someone has been hurt so deeply that they don't think they'll ever be whole again, they're afraid to love—afraid that by opening themselves up again that it will destroy what's left of them. The fact he's here is a good sign."

"I hope you're right."

As they went to leave, Merry called out to them. "Stop." When they did, Merry said, "Look up."

At the same time, they looked above their heads and saw mistletoe hanging there. That was strange; she didn't recall seeing it when she was here before.

Candi lowered her gaze to Michael's. His eyes were dark, and she wasn't able to make out what he was thinking. Her heart pounded. What was she supposed to do now?

Her heart said to go for it. Not giving her mind a chance to talk her out of it, she lifted up on her tiptoes and turned her head so as to kiss his cheek. At the same time, Michael turned his head.

Their lips met. It was like fireworks and the crescendo of an orchestra all at once. It swept her breath away.

Her hands came to rest on his muscled chest. His hands spanned her waist. It was as though time was suspended, and the world faded away. It was just the two of them sharing this delicious kiss.

It started slow, as though they were nervous about where this might lead. She should pull away, but her feet wouldn't work. Her body had a will of its own.

Her heart pounded so loud it echoed in her ears. Could he hear it? Did he know how he got to her?

Michael pulled away, leaving her longing for more. The action caused time to boomerang forward. And she was left a little unsteady on her feet. The kiss had touched her in a way that she'd never felt before.

When she looked at Michael, he appeared flustered. Before either of them were capable of speaking. She struggled to draw air into her lungs.

Had that really happened? When she looked at the color that had bloomed in Michael's cheeks, she knew that it most certainly had happened. What were they supposed to do now?

Buzz. Buzz.

It wasn't her phone. It must be his.

He reached into his pocket and withdrew it. After checking the caller ID, he said, "I have to get this. I'll be outside."

Candi didn't say a word. She couldn't. She was still coming to terms with the kiss.

"No problem," Merry said. "Candi can visit with me."

Michael took long, quick strides toward the door. He moved so fast it was like the building was on fire. Was he that anxious to get away from her? Was he running from the delicious sensations the kiss had evoked?

Then she had a worrisome thought. Did he regret the kiss? Did he wish the kiss hadn't happened? *Please don't let that be the case.*

Candi made her way back to the pups. While she petted them, she talked to Merry about possible homes for the pups. Merry said she had a couple of foster placements in mind for them.

The front door opened. All heads turned in that direction. Michael strode toward them.

His gaze met Candi's before he quickly glanced away. "That was work. I need to go check on a serious issue. There's a buildup of ice, and it's causing problems. I'm sorry to do this, but I shouldn't be long."

Candi couldn't help but wonder if this was a real emergency or if he was grasping for the first excuse he could find to get away from her.

"No problem," Merry said to Michael before turning to Candi. "Would you like to get some hot cocoa? I promise it's the best in the world."

"In the entire world?" Candi smiled as she teased the woman.

"Oh, yes." Merry said it with all seriousness. "Wait until you taste it, and then you can tell me what you think."

She was seriously curious. "Okay. Let's go have some of this cocoa."

When she turned to say something to Michael, she found he was already gone. She felt disappointed that their day together had been interrupted. Not that she was getting attached to him or anything.

Merry slipped on a bright red winter coat with white imitation fur around the collar and wrists. With her snow-white short curly hair, she really did look like Mrs. Claus.

And then Merry put on a Santa hat. *Oh my*! She definitely could play the part of Santa's wife.

"Is something wrong, dear?" Merry gave her a concerned look.

Realizing she was openly staring and her mouth might have gone slack, she glanced away and pressed her lips together. "Um, no. Are you ready to go? After all of that hype, I'm anxious to try that hot cocoa."

"Good." When Merry smiled, her whole face lit up. "Let's go."

With the puppies barking because they hated to be left behind, they headed out the door. Candi had no idea where they were headed, but she instinctively trusted Merry. They only walked a few doors down the road when Merry stopped. "We're here."

Candi turned to take in the red-and-white-striped columns on either side of the front door. They were impressive and looked like giant candy canes. A wooden sign above the door was painted white with red lettering that read: *Kringle Cup Café*.

There was a large picture window next to the door. The tables looked to be filled. It must be a popular place. By the smiles and easy conversation, everyone appeared to be having a good time. It made her all the more curious to go inside.

No sooner had they stepped through the doorway than she heard Merry say, "Hello, Husband."

Candi turned her head in time to catch a man lean over and give Merry a quick kiss. When he straightened, Candi gasped. She blinked to make sure her imagination wasn't getting the best of her.

But as her eyes opened, she still saw Santa. His belly was round with a big black belt around his red velvet coat trimmed with white fur. He had a white beard and mustache. His cheeks were rosy. And behind those gold-rimmed glasses were the friendliest blue eyes she'd ever seen. When he looked at her, it was like he knew who she was, and he knew whether she'd been naughty or nice.

She swallowed. What was wrong with her? There was no such thing as Santa. But the man in front of her challenged that belief.

Merry placed a hand on Candi's arm, drawing her attention. "Candi, I'd like you to meet my husband, Kris Kringle. Husband, this is Michael Bishop's friend, Candi Goodman."

Santa, erm... Kris stepped forward and held his hand out to her. When she placed her hand in his, he gave her a warm shake. "I hope you're enjoying your visit to Kringle Falls."

She noticed he didn't say it was nice to meet her. Was that because he really was Santa, and he already knew whom she was? *No. Of course not.* She just needed something to eat. She should have taken Michael up on that suggestion to eat an early lunch.

Pulling herself together, she said, "I am. It's a wonderful town. I hope to see more of it."

"You should stick around. Kringle Falls has a lot to offer." And then he let out a "*ho-ho-ho*" that sounded so authentic.

"I'd like that." The response was automatic, but after she vocalized it, she realized it was the truth. There was something so welcoming about this small town.

"Oh, there's Holly, Belle, and Felicity," Merry said. "Let me introduce you."

As Candi walked away, Kris Kringle said, "Believe in the joy of the season. It won't let you down."

She wondered what exactly he meant by that, but she didn't stop to ask. She'd already embarrassed herself enough in front of him. But something told her she wasn't the first person to be struck by Kris Kringle's similarities to Santa.

Merry led her over to a table by the big picture window. "This is Felicity Wright, Belle Sinclair, and Holly Berry." As she said each name, they smiled and waved. "Ladies, I'd like you to meet Candi Goodman. She's a friend of Michael's."

Candi noticed how the young women's eyes widened at the mention of Michael. She hoped they wouldn't question her about that. She wasn't ready to discuss Michael with anyone.

"Hi," Felicity said.

"Join us." Belle waved for her to have a seat.

Holly moved over. "Here, sit down."

She noticed that all three of them had something hot to drink. "I'll be right back. I just want to grab something to drink. I heard the cocoa is really good."

They all nodded in agreement.

When she got the cocoa, she also got a ham and cheese croissant. Then she returned to sit with her new friends. They were all around her age. And to her relief, none of them questioned her about Michael.

It was nice having people her age to talk to. Something told her that if she were to stay in Kringle Falls, they would grow to become good friends.

CHAPTER SIXTEEN

H E'D FREAKED OUT.

There was no other explanation for it.

Later that day, Michael couldn't stop thinking about kissing Candi. He tried to tell himself it was an accident—that he'd been intending to kiss her cheek—but he couldn't sell that lie to himself. The truth was that he'd wanted to kiss her.

This acknowledgment was causing him to freak out. It didn't help that when their lips met, he'd felt as though the world had slipped off its axis. He felt as though his life was in free fall.

Candi was the first woman he'd kissed since his wife had passed. And she would be the last. He wasn't going to start over with anyone. He wasn't going to risk his heart again.

Ever since the kiss, he'd noticed that she hadn't spoken much. And now that they were home, she was still quiet. Was it the kiss that had her so quiet? Or was she upset about leaving the puppies?

Not able to take the silence any longer, he'd suggested they watch a holiday movie. She declined the offer. He gave it some more thought and then mentioned working on the Christmas ornaments. She told him maybe later. He assumed that was her polite way of saying no.

He knew he should just go his own way and let her be, but he couldn't just walk away. He felt bad for her. Nothing about this holiday was going right for her. She'd been trying to help a friend by driving the puppies to Maine. She'd never expected to get lost in a snowstorm. And then there was the wreck... It still bothered him to think how close she'd come to freezing to death out there. Thank goodness he'd found her and the pups when he did.

Now, she was stuck here with him. It wasn't fair to her that he was severely lacking the holiday spirit. Maybe he should do something to cheer her up—something to put the sunny smile back on her beautiful face. But how?

It took him a few minutes, then he got an idea. He didn't take time to consider if it was a wise move. He just went with his gut.

He stepped into the kitchen where Candi was sitting at the kitchen island, staring at her phone. "Do you want to get a Christmas tree?"

She turned to him with her eyes widened in surprise. "Do you normally get one?"

He hesitated. Then he shook his head. "Not since Evelyn and Noah." He noticed that the more he spoke of them, the easier it was getting to talk about them. "Evelyn always took charge of the decorating. I just did what she told me. And with it just being me, there was no point in putting up a tree."

"We don't have to get a tree."

He noticed she didn't say she didn't want one. "Come on. It'll be fun. Besides, what else are you going to do this afternoon?"

"Michael, really, you don't have to do this."

"Yes, I do." He moved to grab his coat but then hesitated. "I'm going to get one. You might want to come help me. Otherwise, I can't promise it'll be a nice tree."

She rolled her eyes before she smiled. "You aren't going to give up, are you?"

"Nope." He grabbed her hand and gave a gentle tug. "Come on. You know you want to."

"Fine. If I have to..."

He let out a laugh. "Yes, you have to."

He liked that they'd regained their ease with each other after that unexpected kiss. He still couldn't get it out of his mind. When she stepped into the small mudroom, she leaned past him to grab her coat. In that moment, he was tempted to kiss her again. She was only inches away. It'd be so easy to reach out and draw her to him.

And it would ruin the easiness they'd just achieved. It took everything within him to resist the temptation. What was it about her that drew him to her? Whatever it was, he knew he was in trouble. Big trouble.

It wasn't pretty. Not exactly.

It wasn't lush. Not really.

But it was so ugly it was cute.

A couple hours later, Candi stood in the living room and stared at their Christmas tree. They'd cut it down not far from Michael's house. It'd looked better when it was surrounded by other pine trees.

Still, it had promise. *Didn't it?* She looked at it from this angle and that angle. *Perhaps.* A few ornaments here and a few there would help fill in the empty spots.

She couldn't believe Michael had suggested putting up a tree. She wanted to believe this was another sign of him coming out of his shell, but she cautioned herself not to read too much into his actions.

Michael brought some boxes down from upstairs. They were filled with Christmas decorations. As she peered into box after box, she felt as though she were overstepping, even if he was the one offering up the decorations.

She hesitated. "Are you sure you want me to use these ornaments?"

His gaze didn't quite meet hers as he nodded his head. "They aren't doing any good up there collecting dust."

She found a couple of strings of lights. She plugged them in and was relieved when they lit up. She moved to one side of the tree while Michael stood on the other side.

She knelt down to string the lights along the lower branches of the tree. When she went to pass the lights to Michael, their fingers touched. Her fingers tingled. The sensation zinged up her arm and settled in her chest. It sent her heart racing. She wondered if he'd felt it too. She didn't have the nerve to ask him. In fact, it was best to just pretend it hadn't happened.

They continued wrapping the tree in lights until they made it to the top. She stepped back and surveyed their efforts. "See. It already looks better."

"If you say so," he mumbled.

"I do." She stepped back, and her foot landed on something.

It let out a squeaky sound. She bent down and picked up Tank's favorite squeaker toy. In that moment, she was hit with another wave of sadness. She knew asking Merry to find homes for the pups was in their best interest, but why did it have to hurt so much?

As she stared at the toy, her eyes grew misty. Had she made the right decision? Would Merry find them a loving home?

Michael approached her. "They're going to be okay."

"I know." Her voice cracked with emotion. "I just didn't expect to get so attached to them." A tear rolled down her cheek.

He reached out and drew her to him. His arms wrapped around her. She rested her head against his muscular chest. She wrapped her arms around his trim waist. His comfort was the balm to her aching heart. She could stay there in his embrace forever.

The thought startled her. When she pulled back, she lifted her head to look up at him. He looked down at her at the same time. As she stared into his eyes, it was like a spell was cast over her. Her heart pitter-pattered.

His gaze slipped down to her lips before returning to gaze into her eyes. Was he thinking of kissing her again?

His head lowered. Her body leaned toward him as though by magnetic force. Her heart nearly beat so loud it echoed in her ears. Could he hear it? Did he have any clue what his closeness did to her?

His lips hovered ever so close to hers. Her eyes drifted closed as she waited for his mouth to touch hers...

Ding.

For a moment, neither of them moved. It was though neither of them wanted this moment to end. She felt a connection to him that she'd never felt with anyone else.

And then reality sent them jumping back. Heat rushed from her chest up her neck and set her cheeks aflame.

Ding.

"Sorry," he said. "It's my phone."

And the spell was irretrievably broken. When he stepped away to check his messages, she let out a pent-up breath. She was disappointed that the tender moment had ended so quickly. She wanted to feel his lips pressed to hers once more. Because surely his kiss hadn't been as good as she remembered.

When he slipped his phone back into his pocket, she asked, "Do you have to leave?"

He shook his head. "It was just an update on the ice situation. They have everything under control."

"That's good."

"Now about that food..."

"I can make something," she said.

"No. You've done a lot of the cooking. It's my turn. You just stay here and continue decorating the tree. Or watch a movie. I can't promise anything as delicious as you can make, but at least you won't have to cook this evening." And then he walked away.

She'd never had a guy cook her dinner. They had either taken her out to eat or ordered takeout. She didn't know what he was going to make, but she knew whatever it was, it would be memorable. He was definitely raising the bar for any guys that came after him.

What was he doing?

Almost an hour later, Michael stood at the stove, filling two plates with spaghetti and meatballs. He hadn't cooked for anyone since Evelyn and Noah were alive. And to his surprise, it felt good to be doing something for someone else. But then again, Candi wasn't just anyone. She was like a force of nature, who had happened into his life and turned it upside down.

As he grabbed the grated parmesan, his gaze strayed across the now-empty dog bowls. His thoughts turned to Tank. He knew Candi wanted him to keep Tank, but it just wouldn't work—not with his job and everything. He was certain some nice family would adopt him. Instead of the thought making him feel better, it made him feel worse. Because he missed that dog, even if he was a bed hog.

Michael shoved aside the thought. Dinner was ready, and he wanted to eat it before it grew cold. He carried the plates to the living room, where Candi had Christmas music playing as she hung an ornament on the tree.

He placed the plates on the coffee table and joined Candi next to the tree. "Wow. I didn't think I was gone that long."

She turned to him with a puzzled look. "What are you talking about?"

"The tree. You have it all decorated."

She looked at the tree and then back at him. "Not quite."

"It looks really nice."

"Thanks. I wasn't sure which ornaments you would want on it."

"I like what you picked out." As he continued perusing the tree, he noticed three specific ornaments. They were grouped together near the top of the tree.

He continued to stare at the three white ball ornaments. They were personalized with the names of his wife, son, and himself. He was touched that Candi would think to add them to the tree. There was something so special about Candi. She had such a big, caring heart. And if he wasn't careful, he was going to fall for her.

"I couldn't reach to do the top of the tree." Her voice drew him from his thoughts.

"We can do that after we eat. I hope you're hungry, because I made a lot." He ran to the kitchen to grab the napkins and two cans of pop. After they sat down, he handed her a plate. "I hope you like it."

She smiled. "Thank you. It smells delicious. I can't believe you made this so quickly."

"It helps when the sauce comes in a jar, and the meatballs are out of the freezer."

"It doesn't matter how you created the meal. It's the gesture that counts. And I appreciate you making me something to eat." After taking a bite, she said, "I love it. If you hadn't told me this was jarred sauce, I wouldn't have known."

"Well, I did add a bit of this and that to the sauce." He liked to give his food his own little touches. Remembering the cheese, he held it out to her. "Do you want some parmesan?"

She took it and sprinkled some on her pasta.

"How about we watch a movie while we eat?" he asked.

"Sounds good." She reached for her phone. "Just let me turn off the music." She pressed a button, and silence descended over the room.

"And I'll turn off the lights." He moved to the wall and pressed the switch.

Now the only light in the room was the warm glow from the Christmas tree and the fireplace. Perhaps this was cozier than he'd intended, but it was too late to do anything about it—not without making a big deal out of the romantic setting.

He glanced over at Candi as she took another bite of spaghetti. She didn't seem bothered by the intimate setting.

So, he settled back on the couch and used the remote control to turn on the big screen television. "What do you want to watch?"

"A Christmas movie."

Why wasn't he surprised? "I know. We'll watch *Die Hard*."

"I already told you that's not a Christmas movie."

"Yes, it is."

"No, it isn't." She frowned at him. "There's nothing Christmassy about it."

"There's a Christmas tree in it."

She rolled her eyes. "I have veto power, and I say pick another movie."

He sighed. "You're no fun."

"That isn't what you said when I climbed on the back of your snowmobile earlier today."

She did have a good point. "Fine. You're fun sometimes."

She smiled at him. "Better sometimes than never."

"I suppose so." He turned his focus to scrolling through what was on television.

At last, they settled on a royal Christmas movie. He wasn't sure it would be interesting, but the way Candi had gone on about it, he knew it would make her happy, and that was good enough for him.

As the movie played, the fire started to go down, and a chill came over the room, so he grabbed a blanket and draped it over both of them.

The next thing he knew, Candi's head was resting on his shoulder. And by the sound of her deep breathing, he knew she'd fallen asleep. He smiled. Someone had worn themselves out that day. No sooner had the thought come to him than he yawned.

CHAPTER SEVENTEEN

H ER EYES FLUTTERED OPEN.

Candi glanced around, trying to gain her bearings. The room was dark except for the glow from the television. It took her a moment to realize she was in Michael's house. And her head was resting on his shoulder.

She immediately sat up straight. *How had this happened?* And then she noticed there was a blanket draped over them. The other thing she noticed was that Michael was sound asleep. The poor guy. He was so wiped out.

She should wake him so he could sleep in his own bed, but she hated to disturb him. Maybe it was best to just leave him asleep there on the couch.

She carefully got off the couch, trying not to disturb him. And then she tiptoed to her bedroom. She grabbed one of the pillows from her bed and placed it on the end of the couch.

She thought about repositioning him, but she was certain it would wake him, and he looked so peaceful in his sleep. She grabbed the remote and turned off the infomercial trying to sell an automatic doughnut maker. And then she turned off the tree lights, shrouding the living room in darkness.

Michael made a sound, and then he shifted positions. When she crept nearer, she found him stretched out on the couch. Then he resumed his deep breathing.

With a little smile pulling at the corner of her lips, she tiptoed to her bedroom.

Dinner with the family.

Sunday morning, Candi tried to get out of the family affair, but Michael said if he had to go to dinner, she did too. When she persisted with all of the reasons she shouldn't go, he said he'd call his mother and tell her they weren't going to be there. Candi didn't like that idea.

She got the impression from his exchange with his mother the other day that Michael didn't go to family dinners very often. Something told her that until very recently he had been spending a lot of time alone.

And he proposed they leave early and swing by the pet shop to see the pups. Now he was playing dirty. He knew there was no way she could turn down that offer.

She rushed to get ready, putting on her nicest sweater. It was navy-blue with white snowflakes. Instead of pulling her long hair back into her usual ponytail, she left it down. With a little bit of makeup, she was ready to go.

However, when they stopped at the pet shop, it was closed, and there was no sign of the pups. She was disappointed not to see them. She wondered if Merry had already found each of them a home. She was really hoping Merry would have hung on to Tank for a little longer to give Michael more time to change his mind.

"I'm sorry," Michael said as they walked back to his pickup. "But this is for the best, right?"

She hesitated. "I suppose. I just miss them."

Once they were seated in the pickup, he said, "Maybe someday when you move, you can get a dog."

"I guess, but I'd have to find a job first." She hadn't meant to say that out loud. She didn't want Michael feeling sorry for her.

"You're out of work?"

"It's no big deal." *Liar.* "After the New Year, I'll continue substitute teaching until I find a permanent position." She didn't want to talk about her problems. "Do your parents live far from here?"

He started the engine. "No. Just a couple of blocks. And you're changing the subject."

She wished he'd quit staring at her and instead start driving. "We're going to be late."

He didn't make any effort to put the pickup into gear. "All this time you've been doing things for the puppies and doing things for me, and you never said that you needed help."

"I don't." She didn't want him to look at her with sympathy in his eyes. "I can take care of myself. I've got a plan." When he continued to sit there, staring at her, in that moment she wanted to fade into floorboards and disappear.

"Candi, if there's anything I can do."

She shook her head. "I've got this." She hoped her voice sounded more reassuring than she felt. "Really. I do."

Michael sat there quietly for a moment before he put the truck into gear and headed off down the road.

—ele—

He wanted to help her.

But how?

Michael didn't have time to formulate a plan, because he'd just pulled into his parents' driveway, which was filled with his siblings' vehicles. It looked like this was going to be a big family affair—exactly what he'd wanted to avoid.

He knew his mother was going to make a bigger deal of his relationship with Candi than it was—than it would ever be. He should warn Candi, but when he turned to her, she'd already alighted from the pickup.

He scrambled to catch up with her. "Candi, I need to warn you that my mother is likely to make a big deal about us being here together."

"I kind of guessed that when I met her at the diner."

"If you don't want to go in, I totally understand." Maybe it wasn't too late to turn around and go home. The thought appealed to him. "We can pick up something to eat and head back to my place."

She stopped and turned to him. Her eyes searched his. "Are you trying to talk me out of having dinner with your family?"

"No." The answer came out too quick to be believed. He sighed. "It's just that... I know how they can be, and I, well, I don't want this to be awkward for you."

Her brows drew together. "Don't you mean you?"

"Me, what?"

"You don't want it to be awkward for you?"

He shrugged. He'd been busted. Bringing Candi home to his family was a bigger deal than he'd let himself believe until now. It was a huge deal, and everyone knew it—most of all him.

Candi stared down at the sidewalk. "If you're embarrassed of me—"

"What?" He couldn't believe what she was saying. "Of course not. Nothing could be further from the truth. You're sweet, thoughtful, kind, and so beautiful."

Her gaze darted up to meet his as her cheeks took on a rosy hue. And then the corners of her mouth lifted. He hadn't intended to say all of that, but now he was happy that he had.

The front door opened. "Michael, get in here," his mother called out. "It's freezing out there."

"Guess it's too late to turn around." Candi marched up the sidewalk.

He was quick to follow her. He sure hoped she knew what she was getting herself into. His family could be a handful, to say the least.

When they stepped inside his parent's two-story colonial home, he found his whole family crowded into the foyer. He rolled his eyes as he inwardly groaned. This was going to be an excruciatingly long meal.

Had he really said she was beautiful?

And sweet? And kind?

Candi's heart fluttered every time she recalled his words. She wanted to hang on to that special moment, but now that she was standing in the foyer of his parents' home, she was confronted with the whole Bishop family. She swallowed hard.

She affixed a smile to her face as she looked at the people staring curiously at her. Her stomach shivered with nerves. She'd lost her appetite long ago.

Maybe Michael had been right about skipping this meal. But she'd been so anxious to learn more about him. Like who did he get those dark mysterious eyes from? And did all of his brothers have that same warm, rich chuckle when they were joking around?

"Okay, everyone," his mother said. "Quit standing around, staring. Parker, finish mashing the potatoes. Justin, carry the food to the table. And, Colin, make sure each dish has a serving utensil."

Without an argument, they disappeared. They were now alone with his parents. Candi didn't know if that was good or bad.

Once their coats were hung up, his mother gave Candi a quick hug. "I'm so glad you're here." And then she turned to Michael. She was quiet for a moment as her loving gaze caressed his face. "You've lost some weight. But we can fix that. I made your favorite, roast beef." And then she enveloped Michael in a warm embrace. This hug went on long enough for Michael to send a pleading look at his father.

His father pressed a reassuring hand to his wife's shoulder. "If you hug him any longer, the food is going to get cold."

Michael's mother released her son, and that was when Candi noticed the sheen of unshed tears in her eyes. "I'm just so happy you're here." She looked at Michael, and then she looked at Candi. "I'm glad you're both here."

"Hey, Mom," Michael said. "Should we go eat?"

Candi could sense he was anxious to get this over with. But she didn't know if it was because he was uncomfortable having her there or if it was guilt because he'd obviously been avoiding his family for far too long. Or perhaps it was a bit of both.

His mother led the way to the dining room where food lined the large table. She turned to them. "First, introductions. Candi, I'd like you to meet my oldest, Parker. He's Kringle Falls's sheriff."

Parker stepped forward and shook her hand. "Hi. You're the one that had the accident out in Reindeer Pass."

She wasn't sure if that was a question or a statement of fact. So, she nodded. "There was a detour. Between the snowstorm and my phone losing its signal, I got lost. Luckily, your brother came along to save us."

Parker nodded. "That's right, you have some puppies."

"They're not mine. I was transporting them to a shelter in Maine that had volunteered to find them homes before Christmas. Well, they had until my accident."

Michael cleared his throat. "And now Merry Kringle has them."

"I'm so grateful to her," Candi said. "She's certain she'll be able to find them their forever homes."

When Parker stepped back, Tricia said, "And this is Colin. He's a veterinarian. So, if those puppies need anything, you'll know where to take them."

Colin stepped forward and shook her hand. "It's nice to meet you."

"It's nice to meet you too."

"And last is my baby, Justin." Tricia beamed at her son.

Justin dramatically rolled his eyes. "Mom, how many times do I have to tell you to stop doing that?" There was a distinct rosy hue to his cheeks. "I'm not a baby anymore, if you hadn't noticed."

Tricia stepped up to him. "It doesn't matter how old you get, you will always be my baby."

Justin rolled his eyes again. And Candi did her best to subdue a smile. She already liked this family.

Justin stepped forward and gave her hand a brief shake. "It's nice to put a face with the name at last."

Well, that was a most curious comment. Her gaze moved to Michael, who was looking everywhere but at her. And then her gaze returned to Justin. "I take it you heard about me."

"Definitely." A mischievous grin lit up his face. "You're all Michael has talked about for the past week."

Really? She wasn't sure what to make of this revelation. When she looked at Michael, there was the slightest bit of color in his cheeks.

When his gaze rose to meet hers, he said, "It's not like that."

She wanted to ask what it was like, but as Justin let out a hearty laugh followed by laughter from his other brothers, their mother ushered everyone to their seats.

It was a formal dining room in hues of cream and deep blue. In the center of the room was a large table. It might actually be the largest table she'd ever sat at. They all easily fit around it.

It was like his parents had been expecting to have a large family that would only grow with time, so they bought the largest table available. She supposed there was something to say about positive thinking.

Throughout the meal of roast beef, mashed potatoes, and gravy with a number of side dishes, the brothers kept good-heartedly teasing each other with stories from their youth. There was laughter, and even Michael loosened up to the point where he was lobbing as many verbal jabs as he received.

She loved seeing this side of him. And it wasn't like she was a bystander during all of this. They included her in their conversations. Why Michael would avoid these warm and friendly people was beyond her? She wished she had a loving family like the Bishops.

CHAPTER EIGHTEEN

EVERYTHING WAS CHANGING...

...for the better.

Monday morning, Michael awoke later than normal. It felt good to get some extra sleep. And since he was on vacation all week, there was no place he had to be. He stretched and leaned back against the pillows.

He thought of dinner the day before. Even though his brothers had succeeded in embarrassing him with their playful banter and stories from his youth, Candi had come to his defense a few times. No one had ever done that before. At one point, his mother chimed in and threatened to pull out the photo albums with all of those embarrassing kid photos. Thankfully, he'd distracted her with a request for dessert—anything to keep those photos out of sight. A man could only take so much good-natured teasing in one evening.

By the end of the dinner, Candi had totally won his entire family over, even his father, who was normally the quieter one. Candi had drawn his father out and had him talking about football. Who knew that Candi enjoyed football? He wondered what else he would find out about her that would surprise him.

Every year, he used up his remaining vacation days for the year early. It meant he worked through the holidays, but he wanted to let the people with families take the time off between Christmas and New Year's. Since he no longer had anyone waiting at home for him, it was easier for him to work during the holidays. It helped take his mind off Christmases of the past and the gaping hole in his heart.

He grabbed a quick shower and dressed. He'd forgotten to tell Candi that he was off work, so when he came down the steps and entered the kitchen, she jumped, spilling her coffee.

"Sorry." He rushed over to grab some paper towels to help clean up the mess. "I didn't mean to startle you."

She moved to the sink to rinse off her hands. "I thought you were at work."

"Normally, I would be, but I'm on vacation this week."

As she dried her hands, she turned to him. "I hope you didn't feel like you had to take time off because I'm here."

He shook his head as he knelt down to wipe up the drops of coffee that had landed on the floor. "No. I had this week planned for a while now."

"Oh." She looked as though there was something she wanted to ask him but decided it was best not to. "Can I make you some breakfast?"

He looked around to see what she'd eaten, but he didn't see an empty plate or anything. "What did you eat?"

She held up her mug. "This is all I need."

"You should be glad my mother isn't around to hear you. She would insist you have a big breakfast with all the trimmings. She says it's the most important meal of the day."

Candi smiled. "She should tell that to my waistline. If I ate three meals a day, I'd never fit in my clothes. But I've been known to make an exception for a blueberry muffin or a breakfast burrito."

"Hm..." He opened the fridge and stared inside. "I'm afraid I didn't pick up any tortillas at the store. But I can run out and get some. It'll only take me a couple minutes."

"What?" She looked shocked that he'd go out of his way for her. "Are you serious?"

With a stoic expression, he nodded. "Why do you seem so surprised?"

"I just didn't expect you to drop everything to run out and get me some food."

"Why wouldn't I? You're my guest, and I don't have anything else that I need to do. Besides, a breakfast burrito sounds good to me. I should probably grab some salsa too."

She smiled. "And cheese. And eggs. And either bacon or sausage, whichever you prefer."

He arched a brow. "Which do you prefer?"

She shrugged. "I like both."

"Both it is."

"Michael, you don't have to buy everything I like." Her cheeks took on a rosy hue. It looked really good on her.

"I'll be right back."

Buzz. Buzz.

He stopped and pulled his phone from his pocket. "It's not me."

She moved to the kitchen island. "It's mine. It's Merry. Maybe she has news about the puppies."

Candi pressed the phone to her ear. "Hi, Merry. How are the puppies?"

He should probably get going, or their breakfast would be more like lunch. He glanced over at Candi once more.

Her eyes widened. "What?"

He noticed how her voice rose. Was that a note of panic in her voice? He stood rooted to the spot in the kitchen until he knew everything was all right.

"Are you sure?" Pause. "It's not your fault. This could have happened to anyone."

What happened? Now he was genuinely concerned. He approached Candi. Was it the puppies? Or had something happened to Kris?

"No, I haven't. But Michael is going into town, I'll get a ride with him and have him drop me off. Please, don't worry. We'll figure this out."

Figure what out? He didn't like this not knowing. He wished she would get off the phone and tell him what was going on.

"Yes. I'll keep an eye out. I'll see you soon." At last Candi disconnected the call.

"What's going on?"

Candi put the phone in the back pocket of her jeans. "It's Tank."

His stomach sank. If anything happened to that adorable dog, he would never forgive himself. "What about him?"

"Merry took him outside this morning. She didn't put the leash on him because her backyard is fenced in. When the phone rang, she went back inside to grab it. She was only gone a minute, and when she went back outside, Tank was gone."

He sighed. "That dog's name should be Houdini."

"I agree. She's looked everywhere around her house, but the neighbors haven't seen him. She's very worried, so I told her I would come help her look for him."

"Grab your stuff. I'll meet you in the pickup."

Candi held up a finger as though she'd had a thought. She opened a kitchen cabinet and pulled out a bag of treats. "I forgot about these when we took the pups into town. I've been meaning to give them to Merry. All three of the pups love them but most especially Tank."

"Good idea." Michael moved to the mudroom and put on his snow boots and winter coat.

After grabbing her purse, she rushed into the mudroom. "I'm almost ready."

"I'll start the truck." He headed out the back door.

When he got into the pickup, he decided that under the circumstances, he should loop in his family. They had a family chat link where everyone posted if they needed to contact the whole family. It was so much easier than having to call everyone and repeat the same information.

He pulled it up and started to type:

One of the puppies Candi was caring for has run away. Last seen at Merry Kringle's house. Escaped out of the back yard. No sign of him since.

Then recalling that he had taken some photos of Tank, he flipped through them and attached one of Tank in his bed.

Mom: *Oh no. I'll head over to Merry's.*

Dad: *I can drive around and look.*

Parker: *I haven't seen him, but I'll keep an eye out.*

Colin: *I'm at work, but I'll get the word out.*

Justin: *I'm the closest. I'll start looking.*

Candi climbed into the pickup. "Sorry. My phone rang as I was going out the door. Merry wanted a picture of Tank, and would you believe that I don't have any?"

He noticed the sad look on her face. "Don't worry. This is all going to work out." He reached for his phone. His fingers moved rapidly over the screen. "I just sent you photos of Tank."

Ding. Ding. Ding.

His phone was blowing up with messages. He glanced down to read them. "Do you have to go to work?"

He set the phone in the cup holder before he wheeled the pickup out of the driveway. "Why would you think that?"

"Because every time your phone starts going off like that, it means something has gone wrong, and you have to fix it."

He reached over and placed his warm hand over hers. "I'm not going anywhere until we find Tank. My phone is going off because my family is throwing out ideas of where Tank might be hiding."

"I really appreciate their help."

When he glanced over at her, he spotted her swiping at her eyes. Her tears tore at his heart. All he wanted to do in that moment was fix this for her, but he didn't have a clue where the pup would go. At one point, he released her hand. He reached out and turned on the radio. Christmas music was playing. He knew how much she enjoyed it. Maybe it would help comfort her.

"Why did you turn that on?" she asked. "I didn't think you liked Christmas music."

"I don't dislike it. And I know how much you enjoy it. I thought maybe it would make you feel a little better." He took her hand in his again. This time he was the one that threaded his fingers through hers.

Ding. Ding.

His phone continued to go off.

"Do you think someone found him?" There was a note of hope in her voice.

Michael pulled up to a stop sign. He checked his rearview mirror. There wasn't anyone behind them.

He held his phone out to her. "May I see your phone again?"

Without a word, she handed it over. His fingers moved rapidly over the screen. Then he returned it to her.

"What did you do this time?"

"I added you to our family loop. Now you'll see all of the updates as they come in."

"Thank you." She looked down at her phone. "Your mom is at the Kringles' place. She searched the yard. He hasn't returned."

Ding.

"Colin says everyone at the vet clinic is going to start searching."

"Good. You should look out the window. I highly doubt he would make it this far, but you never know."

"Oh. You're right." She lowered her phone to her lap and stared out the window. "He'll be all right, won't he?"

"Yes." Michael had to believe it.

He put his hand over hers. He noticed how she turned her hand over and threaded her fingers through his. He told himself it was just the worry that had her clinging to him.

She wasn't the only one who was worried. Luckily, it had been sunny all weekend, so some of the snow had melted. Still, if anything happened to Tank, he wouldn't forgive himself. He knew how ornery the dog could be. He should have warned Merry, instead of distancing himself and letting Candi deal with it all.

Where are you, Tank?

CHAPTER NINETEEN

THIS WAS AWFUL.

Candi couldn't believe with what felt like half of the town searching for Tank that no one had found him. They'd been searching for hours.

And now it had started to snow again. She knew the bad weather was going to make the search so much harder. But she wasn't giving up. She didn't care how long she had to walk the streets of Kringle Falls. She was going to find Tank.

"Candi"—Michael's voice had a worried tone to it—"you have to take a break."

"No." She shook her head. "He's out here somewhere. He's probably scared. I have to find him. He's my responsibility."

Michael reached out, gently grasping her forearm. "You aren't going to do him any good if you make yourself sick. You've been out here for hours. The temperature is dropping, and the snow is getting heavier."

She couldn't believe what he was saying. "You want to stop now when he needs us most of all?"

"No. But you need some hot food and warmer clothes."

She wanted to argue with him, but he was right about the clothes. As the frigid wind picked up, it cut right through her jeans. Perhaps the snow suit he'd lent her for the snowmobile would be better.

Reluctantly, she said, "Okay. You go get the clothes, and I'll keep looking."

"No. You have to warm up before you get frostbite." There was a hard edge to his voice, as though he weren't about to negotiate about this point. "Once we change into something warmer. Eat something hot. And get some flashlights, we'll come back out."

She didn't want to go with him—not without Tank. Still, her body was freezing. And her teeth were chattering. So, she grudgingly walked with him to the pickup.

In the pickup, he messaged his family that they were taking a short break. Candi read the group chat that she was now a part of, even though she hadn't contributed to any of the conversations. His mother said she had a big pot of beef vegetable soup on the stove. Michael told her they'd be over shortly.

Candi felt guilty for sitting in a warm truck and going home, *erm*, to Michael's place to put on warmer clothes. All the while, Tank was out there in the snow and ice.

"Hey." Michael's voice drew her from her troubling thoughts. "He's going to be all right."

"It's been hours. He must be frozen."

"You and I both know how smart he is. I'm sure he's found a dry, warm spot to stay until we find him."

"You don't know how much I want to believe that." All the while she stared out the window for any sign of the little pooch. They just had to find him.

*

She did have a point.

And Michael didn't like it. The more time that had gone by, the more he worried about the puppy. Was it possible someone had seen him, thought he was homeless, and took him home?

He didn't like the thought of not seeing Tank again, but if someone cared that much, surely they would give him a good home. It had to be something like that; otherwise, how had Tank disappeared without a trace?

Ding.

His phone had been going off with notifications from his family throughout the day. A couple of times they thought they had spotted him, but the first time, it was the wrong dog, and the second time, it was the fluffy tail of a squirrel. He didn't even ask how Parker had mixed up a squirrel's tail with a dog's tail.

"It's your brother—"

"Which one?" Michael slowed and turned into his driveway.

"Oh. Um, Justin. He says he has searched in the area around the Kringle's house, and he didn't find Tank." Her voice cracked with emotion. "What are we going to do? He needs us."

Michael reached over and squeezed her hand. They'd been holding hands a lot that day. Sometimes for reassurance. Other times just because it felt natural to hold on to her.

"Michael!"

The excited tone of her voice startled him. He pulled his hand back and automatically turned off the engine. "What's wrong?" He didn't hear a notification on their phones, but perhaps he'd been too lost in his thoughts. "Did someone find Tank?"

"Yes." She stared straight ahead.

His heart beat faster. This is what they'd been waiting for. "Where is he?"

She pointed straight ahead.

He turned and looked out the windshield but he didn't see anything. "I don't see him."

"He's crouched in the corner of the porch."

Michael didn't say anything else as he flung open the door. Not slowing down to close it, he jogged up the walk to the porch. When he saw Tank hunkered down in the corner, he couldn't tell if the pup was alive or not. He didn't notice any movement from the puppy.

Using a soft voice, he said, "Tank?"

There was no reaction to him calling his name.

Michael started to make his way across the porch. He took slow, steady steps.

"Is he all right?" Candi called out behind him.

"I don't know." His empty stomach knotted up as he came to a stop.

Was the pup breathing? Michael hesitated to reach out to Tank. Maybe he didn't want to know. He'd already lost too many people who he'd loved. He couldn't lose someone else.

In that moment, he willed the puppy to move. He willed him to fight because he still had his whole life ahead of him. And then Tank lifted his head.

Michael blew out a pent-up breath. His heart leapt in his chest. And his eyes grew misty. It must be from the cold air.

He rushed to the puppy's side. "Oh, Tank. You must be so cold."

He noticed the puppy didn't stand up. So, he scooped him up and held him to his chest.

With his free hand, he reached into his pocket, but his keys weren't there. Where were they?

As though Candi had read his mind, she held up the keys in front of him. "Are you looking for these?"

"How?" And then he remembered leaving them in the truck. "Can you open the door?"

She quickly unlocked it and then pushed the door open. Michael rushed past her. Not bothering to take off his boots, he rushed into the living room. He grabbed the blanket from the back of the couch. He sat down on the couch and wrapped the blanket over Tank and himself.

He looked up at the concerned look on Candi's face. "Call Colin. Tell him we need a house call."

"How do I reach him?"

"The family chat."

"Oh, yeah." She reached into her pocket and pulled out her phone.

Her fingers moved rapidly over the screen. It seemed like she was writing a short story instead of a quick message.

Ding. Ding. Ding. Ding.

Their phones were blowing up with messages. But he wasn't letting go of Tank to check his. "Anything from Colin?"

"Let me see. There are lots of cheers. And sighs of relief. And many questions about how Tank is doing." She was quiet for a moment. "Wait. Here it is. Colin said he has one more appointment, and he'll be right over."

"That better be a really quick appointment."

"I'm sure your brother knows this is urgent. He'll be here as fast as he can. What can I do?"

"I don't know. I'm hoping Tank is absolutely exhausted, and that it's not something more that has him so lethargic."

She sat down next to him. "He's going to be okay." She gently ran a hand over Tank's head. "Aren't you, boy?"

"Can you hold him for just a moment?"

"Sure." She slipped off her coat and sat back on the couch.

As carefully as he could, Michael transferred the puppy to her. He took off his coat and then he started the fireplace. Then he got Tank a bowl of water and some food. Tank wasn't interested in the food but he did drink some water.

As time went by, Michael said, "Where is Colin? What is taking him so long?"

"He'll be here. It hasn't been that long."

Michael raked his fingers through his hair. Every second felt like a minute. Each minute felt like an hour.

He settled back on the couch and held Tank to his chest. He'd only been this scared one other time—when he'd gotten a call that his wife and son had been in an accident. By the time he'd gotten to the hospital, it had been too late. He never got to tell them goodbye.

He petted Tank's head. That wasn't going to happen again.

ele

He was going to be all right.

Candi felt so much better after Colin had examined Tank. He told them to keep him covered with a blanket until he was warmed up. He said the pup's thick coat had helped him in the cold. But it was a good thing they had found him when they did.

When Candi told Colin that Tank had found his way home, Colin was surprised. He'd heard of things like that happening with dogs and cats, but he'd never witnessed it.

After Colin left, Michael's mother and father stopped by. They delivered hot soup and fresh bread. They didn't stay long. Michael wasn't exactly in a chatty mood. He just kept holding the puppy in front of the fireplace. It was like Michael was lost in his thoughts.

She turned on the television to give him something to watch, but he didn't seem interested. Later, she talked Michael into eating some dinner. Tank drank some more water and ate a little food, but not as much as he usually wolfed down. Colin said it might take the pup a little bit to get back to normal, but they were to call if they were worried about anything.

"I can take Tank tonight," she said.

Michael shook his head. "I've got him. I'll take him to bed with me."

"Are you sure? You've been holding him all evening. Maybe you need a break."

"No. I've got this." He started up a couple of steps before turning back to her. "Thanks. Get some sleep."

And then he went upstairs. She watched him go. She felt like something had changed between them since he'd found Tank—like there was once more a distance between them. Maybe it was being out in the cold all day, or maybe he was exhausted.

She didn't want to accept that this wall between them was permanent. They'd been getting along so well. Maybe they all needed a good night's sleep. Tomorrow everything would be all right.

CHAPTER TWENTY

S LEEP HAD BEEN SPARSE.

Michael yawned Tuesday morning as he poured himself some coffee. He watched as Tank ate his breakfast, which Michael's parents had dropped off with the soup the prior evening.

During the night, Tank had stayed under the covers for just a little bit. He preferred to lay on top of them while pressed up against Michael.

Thinking of how close they'd come to losing Tank had dredged up a lot of painful memories. During the night, Michael's nightmares of losing his family came barreling back at him. It'd been a while since they'd tormented him.

This whole experience had reminded him of why he'd closed himself off—because the price of love was just too steep. When he lost someone he cared about, he lost a piece of himself.

He thought of Candi and Tank. It would be so easy to let them into his life—to love them—but he couldn't allow himself to do that. He couldn't take the risk of experiencing the devastating pain again.

Michael turned his attention to Tank. He wasn't his usual energetic self, but after such a huge adventure for such a little guy, it was understandable. Other than that, you couldn't tell anything had happened to him.

Candi entered the kitchen with a smile on her face. "Good morning."

He mumbled, "Morning."

She arched a brow as unspoken questions shone in her eyes. Then she knelt down next to Tank. She ran her hand down over his back. "And how are you today?"

As though the dog understood what she'd said, he turned his head to hers and licked her cheek. She hugged him, and the dog patiently let her.

When she straightened, she moved toward the coffeemaker. She poured herself a cup. "He's looking good. Did you get any sleep last night?"

He couldn't help but wonder if she was asking out of curiosity or if he looked that bad. "A little bit. Tank snores."

"Poor Tank." She fussed over him. "Tell him you don't snore." After another doggy kiss, she moved to the fridge to get some milk for her coffee. "He was just a tired pup. He worked hard to get back to you."

Tank moved to sit next to him. Michael had the urge to bend over and pick him up, but he resisted the temptation. He couldn't risk getting anymore attached to the dog or the beautiful woman standing on the other side of the kitchen island from him.

She added some sugar to her coffee and gave it a stir. "You're going to keep him, aren't you?"

The word *yes* rushed to the back of his throat. He bit it back. Not trusting his mouth, he merely shook his head.

Immediately, he saw the disappointment in Candi's eyes. He couldn't stand to have her look at him like he was the Grinch, who had stolen all of the toys from under the Christmas tree.

He wasn't a bad guy. He'd just suffered through too much loss. He supposed some would say he was broken on the inside. He wouldn't argue with that assessment.

As the awkward silence stretched out between them, he felt as though he needed to say something. "He'll find another home—a good home. It'll be better for him."

Because he didn't know if he had it in him any longer to be the loving, caring person that Candi and Tank deserved. They would be better off without him.

When he turned to walk away, she said, "That's it. You're not even going to try and make a home for Tank?"

"Trust me. It's for the best." It felt as though the weight of the world was pressing down on his shoulders.

And then Tank's wet nose touched his hand. Michael looked down at the pup. His vision grew misty. He blinked repeatedly. Must be dust in the air. He never was that great of a house cleaner.

"You're going to regret this. Tank loves you. You belong together."

She was probably right. And yet the wall he'd built around his cracked heart to keep those jagged pieces together wouldn't allow him to risk love again. Another loss and his heart would shatter into a million tiny pieces—too small to piece back together.

With his head hanging low, he continued toward the mudroom. When he slipped on his boots, Tank joined him.

As Michael petted him, he said, "It's okay. You don't have to go back today. Tomorrow will be soon enough."

She'd heard him.

She'd heard the pain in his voice.

Candi had trailed Michael as far as the mudroom. She wanted to talk some sense into him. But when he went out the door, presumably to go to the workshop, she didn't follow.

She knew deep in her heart that Michael and Tank belonged together. And she was starting to suspect that she and Michael belonged together too. But if he wouldn't let a sweet dog into his life, he was never going to make space for her.

The acknowledgement hurt. It poked at her heart as tears stung the backs of her eyes. Why did he have to be so stubborn?

He wasn't just hurting himself but those around him who cared for him. *Foolish, foolish man.*

She thought about going to the workshop to paint some more ornaments, but she was too angry with him to be in the same room with him. It was best that they kept their distance from each other for the moment.

She glanced out the window to find the sun peeking out from behind the many clouds. She wondered how Odie and Tater Tot were doing. She thought of going to see them, but that would mean borrowing Michael's pickup.

Should she ask him? She worried her bottom lip. She paced back and forth in the living room as she debated what to do. At last, she decided the worst he could say was no.

So, she slipped on her boots and rushed over to the workshop. Michael was cutting more ornaments while Tank slept on a rug near the wood stove. Tank lifted his head and looked at her before going back to sleep.

She waited until Michael finished cutting the wood. "I wanted to go see the pups."

Before she could ask her question, he said, "You can borrow the truck." Then he frowned. "Do you know how to drive a manual transmission?"

She straightened her shoulders and nodded. "I learned to drive in a five-speed." When his eyes widened in surprise, she said, "My mother taught me. She said it was a useful skill to have."

He reached into his pocket and pulled out his keys. He tossed them to her. "There should be plenty of gas in it."

"Thanks." She noticed he didn't offer to go with her. "I'll be back later."

"Take your time."

As she walked away, she wondered if that was his way of telling her he didn't want her around. Was he pushing her out of his life too? The thought saddened her more than she'd expected. But she didn't let any of that stop her from her mission.

It took her a moment to familiarize herself with where everything was on the dash. Then she put her feet on the brake and clutch before turning the key. The pickup immediately turned over. So far so good.

Now if she could just get the pickup out of the driveway without popping the clutch. Her stomach shivered with nerves. She didn't want to embarrass herself after she told him she could drive it. She could do it. It was just that it had been a few years, maybe more than a few years, since she'd worked a clutch and stick shift.

Taking her time so as not to make a mistake, she checked her mirrors. She adjusted the one. With her foot still on the clutch, she put the truck in reverse. She let off the brake and then the clutch. When she released the clutch too quickly, the truck sputtered. She quickly pressed her foot down on the clutch once more. *Slower this time.*

That worked. She backed onto the two-lane country road. When she went to shift into first gear, she saw Michael out of the corner of her eye. He was standing just outside of the workshop. He must have come out to make sure she knew what she was doing with his little red pickup.

Once she shifted, she pressed on the gas pedal and set off down the road. She supposed driving a manual transmission was a lot like riding a bike. You never truly forget how to do it.

As she accelerated, she easily shifted into second and then to third without so much as grinding the gears. Her mother would be proud of her.

Seeing as though the roads had some snow and ice on them, she kept her speed reduced. She wasn't taking any chances with Michael's truck.

Since it was a short ride, she was in town in no time. She found a parking spot near the pet store. Luckily, she didn't have to shimmy into a spot. She wasn't sure she felt confident enough to parallel park. There were a couple of spots open, so all she had to do was drive straight into it.

Before she got out, she decided to call the garage that was working on the van. She hadn't bothered them because there had been no pressing need to have it back...until now.

She felt a seismic shift between her and Michael. Whatever she'd let herself believe was happening between them was definitely over—if it had even really started.

She dialed the number on the business card for the garage. The phone rang and rang. She was starting to think that no one was going to answer it.

"Stan's Garage. Stan speaking."

"Hi, this is Candace Goodman. I was calling about my van."

"Oh, yes. I was going to give you a call a little later."

Her chest tightened. "Is something wrong?"

"No. Actually, I was going to let you know that your van should be ready to go by lunchtime tomorrow."

She would be relieved to have the van back and not having to be reliant on Michael any longer. At the same time, she was sad because this meant there was no reason for her to stick around Kringle Falls any longer.

The man told her that he'd give her a call tomorrow when it was ready to be picked up.

She thanked him and then hesitated. She thought about calling Michael to let him know the news, but then she thought about how cold and distant he'd been since they'd found Tank. She'd tell him later. She dropped her phone into her purse and proceeded to get out of the pickup.

As she walked along the sidewalk, people smiled and greeted her. Most of them she'd never seen before, but that didn't stop her from returning their greeting. Kringle Falls was a warm and wonderful small town. Maybe someday she'd return for a visit.

When she reached the store, a sheriff's car swung over to the side of the road. The window lowered, and she heard someone call her name.

She moved toward the car and bent over to see Parker in uniform sitting behind the wheel. "Hi."

"I thought I saw my brother's pickup. Is he already inside?" He nodded toward the pet store.

"Actually, he's at home. I'm here alone." She held up the key ring. "He loaned me the pickup."

Parker's eyebrows rose as his eyes widened. "He doesn't let anyone drive his baby."

"Really?" She didn't remember him saying anything about it. "Surely, he lets his family borrow it."

Parker shook his head. "I've never driven it. Not even Evelyn drove it. The only person in our family that has had it out on the road is our father, but that was when the pickup still belonged to our grandfather."

Interesting. Why would Michael trust her so much? Probably because he was desperate to get rid of her. It just affirmed her belief that tomorrow it was time to hit the road. She'd worn out her welcome in Kringle Falls.

"How's Tank doing?" He didn't seem in any rush to get going.

"Good. Michael is keeping an eye on him today, before he brings him back to be adopted by someone else." It hurt her to say those words because she knew Tank would never be happy without Michael. She wasn't so sure Michael would be happy without Tank either. But he was too stubborn to realize it.

"I'm glad you guys found him."

"Actually, he found us. Somehow, he made it back to the house. I don't know how."

"Sounds like he's bonded to you."

"Not me. It's your brother that he loves. Only Michael is just too stubborn to admit that he loves the dog too. I don't know why he keeps putting up a wall." And then realizing that she was venting to Michael's brother, whom she didn't know all that well, she pressed her lips together to keep from saying anything else about Michael. "I'm sorry. I shouldn't have said that."

"Don't be. Our family has been tiptoeing around him ever since"—he paused—"well, you know. Anyhow, maybe you're exactly what he needs to draw him out of his shell and start living again."

Just then his radio went off. The Wilkersons' cows were in the road again.

"Sorry," he said. "Duty calls. Call me if you need anything."

"Thanks."

And then he was off. She liked Michael's family. They were all so nice.

She just hoped they weren't counting on her being able to draw Michael out of his shell. She'd failed miserably. And now it was time to get back to her life in Ohio—even if she still hadn't found a new job, and the shelter where she volunteered had shut down. But she didn't want to think about any of that now.

She headed toward Purr 'n Woof. It was time to go say goodbye to Odie and Tater Tot. As she opened the door, she knew this was going to be hard. Who knew she would come to love them so much in such a short amount of time?

There were a handful of people in the store. And some teenager was working the cash register. But Candi didn't see Merry anywhere. Maybe she was in the office.

Candi made her way toward the back of the shop where the fenced-in area was for the dogs. But when she looked inside, she didn't see either of the pups. Maybe Merry had them with her.

Candi walked to the office and found the door open. She peered inside. Merry had her back to her. Candi rapped her knuckles against the door.

When Merry turned, her face lit up with one of her warm smiles. "Candi, it's good to see you. How is Tank doing?"

"Good. He's sticking to Michael's side."

Merry nodded. "At last, they've bonded."

"You would think so, but it seems to be one-sided."

"How so?"

"Well, Michael is determined to bring Tank back here so he can be adopted. I just don't understand it. I know he cares about Tank. He took him to bed with him last night. And by the looks of Michael today, I don't think he got a wink of sleep."

Merry nodded. "It isn't easy for him to open up his heart again."

"But it's a puppy—a puppy that ran home to him. How can he just turn his back on him?"

"Candi, he hasn't."

"Hasn't what?"

"Turned his back on Tank." Merry sent her a reassuring smile. "If he was that determined, he would have dropped Tank off by now."

Candi shrugged. "He said he wanted to watch him today and make sure he's all right. He's planning to bring him back tomorrow."

"Tomorrow is a long way away. A lot can happen between now and then."

Candi wished she could be as assured as Merry, but she'd witnessed Michael putting up his walls. No one could scale those walls—not even with climbing gear.

"Speaking of tomorrow," Candi said, "my vehicle will be ready to go then, so I'm going to be heading back to Ohio."

"So soon?" Merry looked disappointed. "Couldn't you stay longer? I was hoping to talk you into working here. I could really use a manager so I could free up some of my time."

"It's a very generous offer." And she was so tempted to take the job. Merry was so nice, and Kringle Falls was a great small town. But in the end, it was Michael's small town—too small for both of them. They'd run into each other at every turn. "And I really appreciate the offer. It sounds great, but I... I can't accept. I'm sorry."

"Think about it. I don't need an answer today. If you change your mind, call me."

Candi nodded, even though she knew she wouldn't change her mind. "I just stopped by to thank you for your help with the pups. I really appreciate it. Speaking of the pups, are they around? I wanted to say goodbye to them."

"Oh." The smile slipped from Merry's face. "I'm afraid they aren't here. I placed them in foster homes, which I hope will become permanent homes."

"That's great." Candi forced a smile to her lips because she was happy for the puppies, but she was sad for herself because she was going to miss them so much. "You did that really fast."

"It wasn't hard. I know everyone in town. You actually know the two people fostering the pups. Do you remember Belle and Holly from the coffeeshop?"

Candi nodded. It helped to know they were with people she'd met. "But what will happen to them if Belle or Holly don't want to keep them?"

Merry sent her a knowing smile. "Trust me. I have a knack for these sorts of things. Those dogs are in their forever homes, just like Tank has found his. It might take them a moment to figure this out, but it will happen." Merry turned back to her desk. She grabbed a business card and handed it to Candi. "Take this and feel free to give me a call any time."

Candi accepted the card. "Thanks. I'll do that." She turned away and took two steps before pausing and turning back. "By the way, is there a craft store in town?"

"What sort of crafts?"

"Some thread and ribbon. You know, that sort of stuff."

Merry gave her directions to the Kringle General Store. From what Merry said, it had a bit of everything. Hopefully, it'd have what she needed to make Michael a special gift before she left town.

CHAPTER TWENTY-ONE

THE SILENT TREATMENT.

At least that was the way it felt to Candi.

Michael had stayed in the workshop all evening. He hadn't even stopped to have dinner with her. So, they hadn't talked when she got back from her trip into town. She didn't know whether to be angry or hurt or maybe a little of both. She spent the evening working on her special project.

The next morning, she slept in—sort of. She'd had a hard time going to sleep the night before. She'd tossed and turned until very late, when she finally fell into a restless sleep.

And to make matters worse, she'd gotten up this morning to find Michael and Tank gone. Michael had at least left her a note on the kitchen island:

Went to drop Tank off. Might check in at work. Be back later.

M

Her heart broke for both Tank and Michael. His resistance to open his heart solidified her decision. She walked to her room and grabbed the present she had for him. Would he like it? She hoped so. She placed the wrapped package on the kitchen island.

The van had been so kindly dropped off after they'd learned she didn't have a ride to pick it up. It was so sweet of them. Without any excuses to linger, she knew it was time to go home.

She was sad to leave Kringle Falls. But her things were packed and in the van. And yet she was hesitating—perhaps hoping Michael would come home before she left—which was totally ridiculous. It wasn't like he was going to talk her into staying. If he couldn't commit to a dog, he couldn't commit to a relationship. She was just wasting daylight hours.

Still, he'd saved her from freezing in a wrecked vehicle. He'd given her and the dogs a place to stay. She couldn't leave without thanking him.

So, she reached for the pad of paper that Michael had written his brief note on. She ripped off the sheet he'd written on and then started her own note. When she finished, she placed it atop of the present she'd left for him.

Then it was time to go. Inside the van, she paused. She looked at the snowman that had melted just a little but was still standing tall. She thought of retrieving her scarf, but she didn't want to leave the snowman naked. It was a small sacrifice.

Her gaze moved to the workshop. She thought of all the ornaments just waiting to be painted. She told herself it wasn't her responsibility.

Michael had painted them before her; he would paint them after her.

The truth of the matter was that she didn't want to leave. There was something special about Kringle Falls. She was drawn to this place—and Michael. Tears stung the backs of her eyes. She blinked them away.

It was more than just Michael she would miss. There was Merry Kringle. It was her new acquaintances Belle, Holly, and Felicity, whom she was certain would become friends if they had more time. It was the Bishop family, who made her feel as though she were a part of them. They all filled an empty spot in her heart that she hadn't known existed until now.

With tears blurring her vision, she blinked repeatedly, and then she backed out of the driveway.

She paused on the quiet road and stared at the house. "Goodbye, Michael. I hope you're able to find happiness again."

And then she drove away.

He couldn't do it.

Michael sat in his office, checking his email, which was just an excuse not to go home. Because Candi was there, and he owed her an apology. He didn't know if she would forgive him for blocking her out for the past almost twenty-four hours. He wouldn't blame her if she didn't.

Tank put his big paw on Michael's work boot, as though reminding him he was still there. Not that Michael could ever forget the furbaby who'd snuck into his heart.

When he'd left the house that morning, he'd been intent on taking Tank back to Purr 'n Woof. He'd driven by the store twice but had kept going. Another time, he'd slowed down in front of the store, but Tank had been napping and looked so cute, so he'd kept going.

For his last attempt, he'd actually pulled over into a parking spot. He'd sat there for a good fifteen minutes, thinking of all the reasons he should take Tank into the shop and leave him there. Michael was used to living alone. Tank would shed all over the furniture. But most of all, Michael wasn't ready to open his heart up. He wasn't ready for the risk of losing someone else he loved.

But what finally made his decision was the fact that love wasn't something you planned for. Love wasn't something you could just choose to have in your life when it was convenient. Love came in its own time and in its own way—even when it was inconvenient or unwanted.

You can fight it, but in the end, love wins every time.

And the truth was that he loved Tank. How could he not? The dog was adorable and irresistible.

When he was finally able to admit this to himself, he breathed easier. As he'd driven away with Tank, he knew it wasn't his decision about keeping the dog that had him freaking out.

It was coming to terms with his feelings for Candi. For so long, he'd been able to lie to himself about his growing feelings for her, but he couldn't do that any longer. She was leaving soon, and he had to decide what to do before then.

"What are you doing here?"

Michael was startled from his thoughts. He hadn't heard the footsteps. He looked up from his computer monitor to find Justin standing in the doorway.

Michael cleared his throat. "I, uh, have work to do."

"This is your vacation week. You do remember that you're not supposed to work on your vacation, right?"

"That isn't always the case when you're the boss."

Justin nodded toward Tank. "And I suppose he's assisting you." Justin approached the dog and fussed over him. Tank rolled over and let his brother pet his belly.

"So much for him being a guard dog," Michael said teasingly. "He lets anyone pet him."

"Hey. I'm not just anyone. I'm your favorite brother."

Michael arched a brow. "Favorite, huh? I don't remember ever saying that. Do Parker and Colin know this?"

"They've always known it." Justin sent him a big grin. "So, what are you really doing here? Shouldn't you be with Candi?"

"What's that supposed to mean?"

Justin arched a brow. "Are you trying to tell me that you aren't crazy about her?" When Michael shrugged, Justin continued. "Everyone can see it when you look at her or when you talk about her. They're even taking bets about whether you'll do something about it or let her slip through your fingers."

"Are you serious?" When Justin nodded, he asked, "And how did you bet?"

"Oh, I can't tell you."

"Yes, you can. Or I can tell Mom how you broke her favorite vase when you threw the baseball in the house and let the cat take the blame."

"You wouldn't?" When Michael arched a brow, Justin said, "That's not fair. I was only fourteen at the time."

Michael shrugged. "There's no statute of limitation. So, out with it. How did you bet?"

Justin sighed. "I said you'd blow it with her. Sometimes you're so stubborn that you can't see a good thing, even if it walked up and slapped you in the face."

Michael wanted to argue with his brother, but perhaps there was a note of truth in his words. Instead, he sat there quietly, wondering if he was going to regret it when Candi left. He already knew the answer.

"Listen, big brother, I know how much you've been through. It was the worst, but I just can't see Evelyn wanting you to punish yourself the rest of your life. It's time for you to live again."

Justin didn't wait for a response. He turned and walked away as quietly as he'd arrived. Michael was left alone with his thoughts. His mind told him that letting himself care for Candi was just asking for more heartache. It was safer to leave things the way they were.

His heart told him to race to Candi and tell her that he was sorry for acting like a fool. He should plead for forgiveness and then tell her that he loved her.

Whoa! Wait. Did he love her? He pondered it for a moment.

He did. He loved Candi.

He'd been so busy fighting his feelings for her that he hadn't even noticed when it had happened. He thought of Evelyn. She had been a good woman. His brother was right. She wouldn't have wanted him to be alone the rest of his life. And something told him that if Candi and Evelyn had met under totally different circumstances, they would have been fast friends.

He knew then and there what he needed to do. He got to his feet. "Tank, let's go home."

"Bark. Bark."

A few minutes later, they arrived at the house. Michael was nervous. What if she didn't forgive him? What if she didn't feel the same way?

His empty stomach knotted up. He didn't let it stop him. When he got to the side door and found it locked, he was surprised. Usually it was left unlocked during the daytime.

Using his key, he unlocked the door and stepped inside. He was greeted by silence. He wasn't used to it because as long as Candi had been staying with him, there was either Christmas music playing or the sounds of a holiday movie.

"Candi?" He looked in the kitchen. She wasn't there. "Candi, are you here?" He moved to the living room before looking in her room, but he didn't see any sign of her. When Tank pressed his wet nose to his hand, Michael petted his head. "It's okay, boy. I'm sure she's just out in the workshop painting some ornaments. Let's go find her."

As though he understood what Michael had told him, Tank led the way to the back door. But on the way through the kitchen, Michael noticed the wrapped gift on the island.

When he saw his name on a folded piece of paper, the knot in his gut tightened. He hesitated before picking it up. Something told him he wasn't going to like what it said.

Tank barked at him as though to tell him to hurry up and open it.

Michael's chest tightened as he unfolded the paper and began to read:

Michael,

Thank you for riding to the rescue when we wrecked. You saved our lives, and I will always be grateful. And then you opened your home to us, when you could have just dropped us off in town and drove away. You are such a good man. And I am going to miss you. But it's time that we each get on with our lives. I know how much you love your work. Kringle Falls is lucky to have you. I'll never forget you or our Christmas adventure.

Love,

Candi

P.S. I've left a gift for you. I hope you like it.

His vision grew blurry, and he swiped at his eyes. He was too late. She was gone.

With a heavy heart, he picked up the wrapped package and removed the wrapping paper. Inside, he found another little note and a pillow. It wasn't just any pillow; it had his son's name embroidered on it. It took him a moment, but then he realized this was part of the pillow the dogs had destroyed their first night at his house.

Candi had cut away the damaged parts and turned it into a small square pillow with ribbon and lace around the edge. It was just the right size to put on display on a bookshelf far from Tank's reach.

He stared at it for a moment, touched that she'd gone through so much trouble. She could have easily thrown the ripped material away, but she hadn't.

And then he looked at the note. It read:

We're sorry!

We love you,

Odie, Tater Tot, and Tank

P.S. I'm sorry too. Hope this helps. C.

He looked at the pillow again. How did he let someone so thoughtful, kind, and loving slip through his fingers? He was such a fool.

He reached for his phone and dialed her number. It went directly to voicemail.

He wanted to go after her, but he didn't have a clue what time she had left or what direction she had gone in.

The cracks in his heart widened. The pain stole the breath from his lungs. He'd done everything he could to protect himself from getting hurt, and in the end, he had ended up hurting himself.

Chapter Twenty-Two

ONE LAST LOOK.

Candi drove through Kringle Falls one last time before heading back to Ohio. She didn't want to forget anything about this special little town.

Her heart wanted to seek out Michael and tell him he was a fool for pushing her and Tank away. But her mind told her she had more dignity than that. She couldn't throw herself at a man who obviously didn't want her. And it didn't matter how much she'd come to love him.

She drove slowly past Purr 'n Woof. She was so tempted to pull over and go inside, but she didn't let herself. It would just make leaving Kringle Falls that much harder.

Instead, she pressed harder on the accelerator. She just had to get away from there. Her foot pressed even harder on the accelerator. The farther she got from this town, the better she'd feel. Wouldn't she?

Wee-oow. Wee-oow.

She glanced in the mirror to find flashing red lights. *Just great.*

She looked down at the speedometer to find she was, in fact, ten miles over the posted speed limit. Now she would have a speeding ticket to remember Kringle Falls by.

By now she was outside the town limits. She put on her turn signal and pulled over on the berm of the road.

As her front tire dropped off the asphalt, there was a big pop. The van dipped hard to the right side, but kept moving. What had happened?

She wanted to investigate, but the red flashing lights in her mirror reminded her she had to deal with a speeding ticket. She reached for her purse to get her driver's license.

Tap-tap.

She looked through the window to find Sheriff Parker Bishop standing there. He wore dark sunglasses that kept her from seeing his eyes. She sent him a smile as she rolled down the window. He didn't smile back.

"Do you know that you were going over the speed limit?"

She fumbled through her purse, looking for her wallet. "I'm sorry. I was distracted."

"Distracted by what?"

What was she supposed to say to that? "I... I was just taking one last look around."

"You're leaving?"

She nodded. "It's time."

"Does my brother know this?"

"I..." She finally found her wallet. "I don't know. I left him a note."

He arched a brow. "A note?"

She nodded. "He left this morning before I got up, and he didn't come back by the time they delivered the van." She stopped rambling. Why was she telling him all of this? None of this had anything to do with her speeding. "It doesn't matter. Could I have my ticket so I can get going?"

Parker didn't say anything as he walked around the van, as though he were inspecting it. By the time he made it the whole way around the vehicle, he was frowning. "You aren't going anywhere."

"What are you talking about?"

"You blew out a tire, and if I'm not mistaken, your rim is now bent."

Candi groaned. "What else can possibly go wrong?"

"Stay here. I'll call for a tow." He didn't wait for her to say anything.

She noticed he hadn't said anything about the ticket. Maybe he felt bad enough for her not to give her one. That would be a good thing because with her not working, her savings were dwindling.

She sat there, glancing in the mirror every few seconds. He was certainly taking a long time. She sighed. What was Parker doing? Maybe he was writing up that ticket after all.

She picked up her phone and noticed it was dead. *Really?* She'd been so upset the night before and that morning it hadn't even crossed her mind to charge it.

She sat there, waiting. And waiting. And waiting. What was taking so long?

The next time she looked into her mirror, she saw a very familiar red pickup coming down the road. *Great.* Now she got to be embarrassed in front of the man she loved, who didn't love her back.

Michael pulled over in front of her van. What did he want? They had nothing left to say.

Her window was still down because she thought Parker was going to come back, but instead, he turned off his lights and pulled out.

"I heard you needed some help." Michael leaned his hands against the door.

"I thought your brother was helping me."

"He called me."

"He did?" *That traitor.* "Listen, Michael, I appreciate everything you've done for me, but I've got this. The garage will just put on a new wheel, and I'll be on my way."

"What if I want you to stay?"

She wasn't sure she'd heard him correctly. "What did you say?"

"I want you to stay."

Her heart tap-danced in her chest. "You do?"

He smiled and nodded. "You know it's cold out here. How about we have this conversation in my pickup?"

No sooner had he said it than a familiar tow truck pulled up with its yellow lights flashing. She gathered her things and walked with Michael to his vehicle.

When he opened the passenger door for her, she was surprised by Tank. He leaned over and licked her face. She hugged him. "You're back."

"He never left," Michael said. "I couldn't take him back to Purr 'n Woof."

He closed the door and moved to the back of the pickup. She saw him in the mirror as he spoke to the tow truck driver.

Once Michael was in the driver's seat, he turned to her. "I'm sorry, Candi. I've been pushing you away, and I shouldn't have done that. I hurt you, and I hurt me. And I'm sorry."

"I understand. You didn't want to get hurt again."

"But I did anyway because I was being so stubborn and refusing to admit to the happiness and joy that you've brought back to my life." He looked deep into her eyes. "I love you, Candi."

"You do?" Her heart pitter-pattered. She couldn't believe he was saying all of the things that she'd longed to hear.

His brown eyes searched hers. "I do. Will you forgive me?"

"Yes." A rush of emotions had happy tears welled up in her eyes. "Yes, I will. Because I love you too."

They leaned over the top of Tank, and their lips met. Nothing had ever felt so right. Her heart fluttered in her chest.

When they pulled back, she asked, "How is this going to work?" Then she hesitantly asked, "Are we going to have a long-distance relationship?"

"I've given this some thought, and I don't think long distance will work for either of us." When Tank barked, they both laughed. "It looks like Tank agrees. So, I could look into getting a job near you."

She was surprised by how serious he was about making their relationship work. "You would give up your job and move away from your family?"

He shrugged. "One of us has to be willing to move. I can't ask you to do something that I'm not willing to do. Besides, we can visit my family for holidays and stuff."

Tears rushed to her eyes. No one had ever loved her that much. It made what she was about to say so much easier.

"I don't want you to do that."

Concern shone in his brown eyes. "You don't want us to be together?"

"I want us to be together, but I don't want you to move to Ohio."

"What are you saying?"

"That I'll move to Kringle Falls. Merry has already offered me a job, and I can apply for a teaching position at the school here." When he was quiet, she asked, "You don't look happy about it."

"It's not that. I just want to make sure this is really what you want."

"I want to be wherever you are." When Tank nosed her chin, she laughed. "And where Tank is. If you haven't noticed, I've fallen in love with Kringle Falls. Who wouldn't love a Christmas town?"

"Wait. Does this mean that you're going to make me decorate the outside of the house?"

She smiled at him. "Most definitely."

He groaned and rolled his eyes. "What have I done falling in love with a Christmas-fanatic?"

"Oh. It isn't that bad." She lightly punched his arm. "Maybe my love of the holiday will rub off on you."

"That's what I'm afraid of." Michael put the pickup in gear.

"But I still have to go back to Ohio to return the van and empty my apartment."

"You aren't going alone." Tank barked his agreement, and they laughed. "We don't think you're safe driving alone in that van. So, we've decided to go with you."

"Really?" She hadn't been expecting that. "But what about your work?"

"They can survive without me for a few days. Besides I'm on vacation, remember?"

"So you're going to vacation in Cleveland in December?"

"Yep. I heard it's the place to be. And there happens to be a woman there that I love." He held his hand out to her.

She placed her hand in his, lacing her fingers with his. "I love you too."

CHAPTER TWENTY-THREE

IT WAS TIME FOR goodbye.

Back in Cleveland, Candi sorted everything in her apartment. There were three piles: keep, donate, and garbage. Michael worked to pack up everything she wanted to take with her.

Originally, they'd been planning to rent a car to drive back to Vermont, but once Michael saw how much she had to take with her, they agreed to rent a small moving truck.

He'd offered to let her stay at his place until she found her own apartment. He didn't seem to think finding a place for her to live would be too hard. He already had his mother looking into what was available.

This was the most spontaneous thing Candi had ever done. And even though she was nervous about giving up everything she knew and moving to a new town, she knew deep in her heart it was the right thing to do.

And now they were on their way to meet Bob to return the van. He was at the now-closed animal shelter. He was clearing the place out.

"You're quiet over there." Michael's voice drew her from her thoughts. "Is everything okay?"

She nodded. "I was just thinking about Bob. He's the one person I worry about leaving. He's getting older, and his son doesn't live close by. He's been like family to me."

"You could ask him to move to Kringle Falls."

She nodded. "It's an idea, but I don't think he'll go for it. He can be stubborn when he wants to be." She saw the familiar building come into view. "That's the place up ahead. You can just park in front."

He pulled to a stop behind a blue SUV. They got out, and with Tank on a leash, they walked into the shelter. After more than five years of volunteer work, she couldn't believe this was the last time she would be there. She hoped Merry would consider opening an adoption program in Kringle Falls. She planned to discuss it with her when they got back to Kringle Falls.

"Bob?" Candi called out. Nothing. She tried again. "Bob, are you here?"

"In the office." His words were followed by a string of coughs.

He shouldn't be here. It didn't feel like the heat was on. If it was, it was turned way down. But she knew telling him to go home would be a waste of her time. The man was so stubborn.

But she wondered what he would say when she told him she was moving to Vermont. Would he even entertain the idea of going with her? She hoped so.

She reached out, taking Michael's hand in her own. "It's back this way."

They walked past the empty front desk, through the open doorway that led to the area where they used to house the dogs and cats. Off to the side of the large room was a modest office.

For the first time since she'd volunteered there, she could see the top of Bob's desk. "Looks like you've been busy."

"You're back." He stood up and came around the desk to hug her.

When they pulled apart, she said, "Bob, I'd like you to meet Michael Bishop." She turned to the man of her dreams. "Michael, I'd like you to meet Bob Hoffman."

Bob shook Michael's hand. "It's good to meet you." Bob looked down at Tank. "And it's good to see you again." After he fussed over the dog, his gaze rose to Michael. And teasingly he said, "I hope you're not trying to bring him back. We have a no-return policy."

"Oh, no. He's become my shadow."

Bob nodded. "Animals have a good sense about which humans they bond with. Tank is very particular, so I already know that you're a good man."

When Bob started coughing again, he sat back down. It was then she noticed his face was pale, and there were more lines on his face. It was as if he'd aged ten years overnight.

"Before I forget." Candi reached into her purse and pulled out the keys to the van. She laid them on his desk. "I'm very sorry about the accident."

Bob shook his head. "I'm the one that's sorry. I sent you out in a snowstorm. I'm so grateful that you're okay." His gaze moved to Michael. "I hear that I have you to thank for that."

Michael modestly shrugged. "Just happened to be in the right place at the right time."

"Bob, I have news." Candi sat down in the chair facing his desk. "I'm moving to Kringle Falls, Vermont."

"Vermont?" His eyes widened. "You must have had a really good time there."

Candi glanced at Michael. "I did." Then she turned back to Bob. "And now that you're retiring, I wanted to know if you'd come with me."

His bushy brows rose high on his forehead. "You want me to move to Vermont? With you?"

She nodded. "I do. I think you'd love it there. It's a small town that celebrates Christmas year-round."

"Hey, Dad." A short man with sandy-blond hair stepped into the room with a golden dachshund under his arm. He stopped talking and glanced at her and then Michael. "Sorry. I didn't know you had company."

Candi was surprised. She hadn't missed the part about this man calling Bob "Dad." This was his son? The son that he talked about for years but who never came around?

"Candi and Michael, I'd like you to meet my son, Shaun. He's asked me to move to Tennessee to be near him and his family." Bob made the introductions.

Candi was surprised by this sudden reunion, but she was also very happy for both of them. She knew this was what Bob had wanted for years.

She turned to Bob. "I'm so happy for you. It looks like we're both getting fresh starts."

Bob nodded. "But at least my new home won't be as cold as yours."

"True. But now I have someone to snuggle up to." She turned a grin toward Michael, who was smiling as he shook his head.

"I do have one last favor to ask of you." Bob's expression turned serious.

"Uh, sure." She kind of owed him big time after wrecking his van. "What do you need?"

"Could you find a home for one more dog?"

She glanced over at the dachshund that his son had placed on the floor. Tank was now sniffing him. "You mean this little guy?"

Bob nodded. "Actually, it's a girl. We've been calling her Sunny. We arrived this morning to find this little girl tied to the front door. I can't believe someone would just abandon her. I don't even want to think of what would have happened to her if I was still in the hospital." He let out a deep cough.

Candi worried her bottom lip as she looked at the little dog. She was a cutie. She couldn't imagine it would be hard to find her a home.

"Just give me a moment to make a call." She stepped out of the office to call Merry.

The conversation was a little longer than she'd intended, especially when she took Merry up on the job offer.

Ten minutes later, she returned to the office. "Sorry about that. The answer is yes. We'll take her."

The lines on Bob's face smoothed, as though he were starting to relax. "Thank you, Candi. You're the best."

His son handed over the dog leash. "Here you go."

The four of them talked for a bit before Candi and Michael left. Once they were in the back of a ride share, Tank lay across Michael's lap while Sunny settled on her lap.

She looked over at the man who'd stolen her heart. "Here we go again."

"This time, can we skip getting lost in a snowstorm and going over an embankment?"

"Most definitely. We'll just skip to the kissing." She leaned toward him.

He leaned toward her.

And their lips met in the middle.

Epilogue

CHRISTMAS EVE

He was up to something.

However, she just didn't know what it was.

Candi knelt in front of the Christmas tree and placed the wrapped gifts she'd gotten for Michael under it. They'd decided to do Christmas at his place since he already had a Christmas tree, and she was still moving into her new apartment above Purr 'n Woof.

Not to mention, he had a fireplace to take the chill out of the air. They were going to have a white Christmas this year. It was already snowing outside. It was only supposed to amount to a couple of inches, but that was plenty to coat Kringle Falls in fluffy white stuff.

She used her phone to turn on some Christmas music. This was going to be a perfect evening.

So much in her life had changed in the past few weeks. She loved her new apartment. But talk about living close to your work. She'd never have a legitimate excuse for being late. She didn't think Merry would buy the story that there was a traffic jam on the steps.

Candi knew from talking to Michael's family that they normally opened their presents on Christmas morning. And yet Michael had insisted they open theirs on Christmas Eve. They went back and forth. Candi wanted to wait and open them in the morning. He insisted they had to open them that evening. At last, they came to a compromise—they'd each open one gift on Christmas Eve and the rest of them on Christmas morning. He seemed satisfied with this solution. She had to wonder what he had gotten her that was so special he couldn't wait.

She knew it wasn't going to be a diamond ring. They'd discussed it and it was far too soon for either of them. So, what else could it be?

She had absolutely no idea. And as much as she'd pestered him, he wasn't giving her any hints.

"Hey." Michael stepped into the living room. He looked under the tree and then he frowned at her. "How many presents did you get me?"

She smiled and shrugged. "Not that many."

He arched a brow. "It sure looks like a lot to me. Wait here. I have to go shopping."

She got to her feet and rushed over to him. She took his hand in hers. "You aren't going anywhere."

She'd gotten him some clothes and tools for his workshop. She wrapped every single item individually so it looked like there were more presents under the tree than there actually was. It was something her mother had done for her at Christmas time. Her mother hadn't had a lot of money, so she took what they had and made the most of it.

"Would you come sit down?" she said. "You've been on the go since I got here. What's going on?"

"Nothing." His answer came out far too quickly to be believable.

"Michael James Bishop, what are you up to?" She narrowed her gaze on him, hoping to make him crack.

He smiled and shook his head. "I'm not telling."

"Michael, I know you're up to something." When he grinned, she said, "See I knew it."

"Just trust me. You'll love what I have in store for you."

It was then she noticed Tank was missing. She must have been more excited about this Christmas than she realized for her to miss something like Tank not being around. Usually, he met her at the door.

The smile faded from her face. "Where's Tank?"

"Oh. Um... He's around." Michael tried to look innocent, but she could tell there was something more he was keeping from her.

And then she started to worry. "Please, tell me he's all right."

Michael placed his hands on her shoulders. "Stop worrying. He's fine. I promise. I wouldn't keep something like that from you."

She stared into his eyes until she was certain he was telling her the truth. "Good."

And then he smiled and pointed above his head. In the doorway between the kitchen and living room hung some mistletoe.

She smiled. "I don't remember that being there."

"Well, you said I needed more decorations, so I made sure to put up the most important one."

She laughed. "Most important, huh?"

"Most definitely." He wrapped his arms around her waist and drew her to him. "How else am I going to get more of these?"

He lowered his head and claimed her lips. Her heart pitter-pattered. She definitely approved of the mistletoe.

Before they got too distracted, she pulled back. "We each have a gift to open."

He sent her a pouty look. "We'd have more to open if you'd let us open them all tonight."

She laughed again. "Your mother must have had her hands full with you on Christmas Eve." She moved to the Christmas tree and knelt down to pick up the present she'd chosen for him to open. She straightened and turned to him. "This is for you."

He looked at the package and then his gaze met hers again. "I want to give you my gift first."

"But I already have yours. Open it. Please" She sent him a pleading look.

He accepted the gift and ripped the paper off like a little kid on Christmas morning. She smiled and realized that she'd wasted her time carefully wrapping each gift. He didn't even notice that the folds were perfect or the tape was in the right spot.

Inside was a white gift box. He lifted the lid to find two white glass ball ornaments. On one, his name was painted on one side and the year on the other. The second ornament had Tank's name and the year."

Michael looked in the box, then he lifted his gaze to her. His brows drew together. "Where's the other one?"

"What other one?"

"The one with your name on it."

She smiled. "Michael, you're rushing things. There'll be time for that someday."

He sighed. "Okay. But the day will come when your ornament is up there with ours."

She felt this gift needed an explanation. "These ornaments aren't to replace the ones you have with your wife and son's names, but rather to expand your family."

His eyes grew misty. He blinked repeatedly. "Thank you. I never received such a thoughtful gift."

He leaned down and pressed his lips to her. It was a sweet, tender kiss.

When he pulled back, she said, "I understand and respect that the memory of your wife and son will always have a place in our lives. Any time you want to talk about them, I'm more than willing to listen."

His gaze searched hers. "It wouldn't bother you?"

"Should it?"

He shook his head. "I'm learning that the heart has a great capacity for love. I have plenty of love for them and you too."

"I love you too."

He reached out and pulled her into a warm embrace. Her head came to rest on his chest. She heard the steady thump-thump of his heart. How did she ever get so lucky to have him in her life?

He pulled back and said, "Now it's my turn to give you a gift." He took her by the shoulders. He guided her backward until the back of her knees hit the couch. "Sit here and no looking around. Okay?"

She sat down. "You're being very mysterious."

He grinned at her. "Yes, I am."

And then he walked away. *What is he up to?* And then she heard the back door open and close. Then there was more silence.

She knew she wasn't supposed to peek, but she was so curious. She turned to the side and peered back toward the kitchen. She didn't see Michael or anything that looked like a present.

Suddenly, the back door opened, and Michael peered inside. His gaze met hers. "You're cheating. Turn around."

She huffed as she turned around. "What are you up to?"

"Close your eyes."

"Michael?"

"Close your eyes and keep them closed if you want your surprise."

She closed her eyes. She tried to guess what he was up to, but she didn't have a clue.

And then she heard Tank's nails tapping on the kitchen floor. What did it have to do with him? And why did it sound like he was running around the kitchen?

And then she heard them approach her. She was tempted to peek, but she resisted the urge.

"Okay. You can open your eyes."

She had her eyes open before he finished saying okay. Sitting before her was not one but two dogs. She was confused. Right beside Tank was a white boxer.

"And who is this cutie?" She lowered her hand so the dog could sniff her.

"This would be your dog. And before you say anything, I know you were waiting to have your own dog until you had a place that allowed dogs and you wanted one that was special—that other people had passed by. Well, Snow here has a long sad story. She was adopted and returned three times for being deemed untrainable."

Her heart melted for the dog. "But I don't understand. She seems so friendly and well-behaved."

"According to Bob... And before you ask, yes, he's been helping me find the perfect dog for you. Anyway, according to Bob, it was just discovered that Snow is deaf. So she's going to need some extra love and care. Do you think you're up for the task?"

She wanted to reach out and give Snow a great big hug. She resisted the urge. She didn't want to scare the dog.

She looked up at Michael and smiled at him. "How did you know I was ready to adopt?"

He shrugged. "You might have mentioned it once or a hundred times."

She laughed. "Hey, I'm not that bad."

She slowly moved her hand to pet Snow. She wasn't skittish, so that was a plus. Now Candi had to do a lot of research about how best to care for a deaf dog. She had some experience with them, but she was certain she had more to learn. She didn't want to fail Snow.

When Tank moved to walk to the kitchen, Snow shot away from Candi in order to follow him. Candi was impressed with the way the two dogs got along.

"Snow seems to have bonded with Tank." She stood so that she could watch the duo.

"Over the past few days that I've had her, they've really warmed up to each other."

She arched a brow as she looked at him. "Is this why you've been so busy lately that I've hardly seen you?"

"Guilty as charged." His gaze moved to the dogs. "Do you like your gift? Because if you don't want a dog right now, Bob said he'd find Snow another home."

"Oh, no. I love Snow. If she's a buddy of Tank's, I know that she's a good dog with a big heart because Tank is very particular about who he hangs out with."

Michael smiled. "Does that mean I'm also good and have a big heart?"

"Well..." she teased.

He pulled her into his arms. "Hey, that's not nice."

She tilted her chin upward and stared into his eyes. "You're the best man I know, and you have a heart of gold. No one has ever given me a more meaningful gift. This is the best Christmas ever. I love you."

"I love you too." He leaned down and pressed his lips to hers.

Keep reading Candi and Michael's story! Sign up for my newsletter and receive a bonus epilogue. Get your bonus epilogue HERE.

And then return to Kringle Falls to read about the next Bishop brother to find love. Sheriff Parker Bishop follows the rules and expects those around him to follow them too. Except there's one redhead in town who's forever testing his patience. Belle Sinclair thinks rules are suggestions, and laws are for bending. Talk about mixing oil and water. Oh my! It's Odie's turn to find his forever home. This Christmas, these two enemies will have to work together to help this special little dog in PUPPY LOVE & SNOWFLAKE KISSES.

Afterword

Thanks so much for reading Carrie and Michael's story. I hope their journey made your heart smile. If you did enjoy the book, please consider...

- Help spreading the word about PUPPY WISHES & CANDY KISSES by writing a review.
- Subscribe to my newsletter in order to receive information about my next release as well as find out about giveaways and special sales.
- You can like my author page on Facebook.

I hope you'll come back to Kringle Falls and read the continuing adventures of its residents. In upcoming books, there will be updates on previous couples as well as the addition of some new visitors to the islander.

Coming next is Belle Sinclair & Sheriff Parker Bishop's story in PUPPY LOVE & SNOWFLAKE KISSES.

Thanks again for your support! It is HUGELY appreciated.

Happy reading,
Jennifer

ABOUT AUTHOR

Award-winning author, Jennifer Faye pens fun, heartwarming contemporary romances. With more than a million books sold, she is internationally published with books translated into more than a dozen languages and her work has been optioned for film. She is a two-time winner of the RT Book Reviews Reviewers' Choice Award, the CataRomance Reviewers' Choice Award, named a TOP PICK author, and been nominated for numerous other awards.

Now living her dream, she resides with her very patient husband and two spoiled cats. When she's not plotting out her next romance, you can find her curled up with a mug of tea and a book. You can learn more about Jennifer at www.JenniferFaye.com

Subscribe to Jennifer's newsletter for news about upcoming releases, bonus content and other special offers.

You can also join her on Facebook, or Goodreads.

Also By

Other titles available by Jennifer Faye include:

BLUESTAR ISLAND:

Love Blooms

Harvest Dance

A Lighthouse Café Christmas

Rising Star

Summer by the Beach

Brass Anchor Inn

Summer Refresh

A Seaside Bookshop Christmas

A Lighthouse Snapshot

Inheriting Her Island House

A Brass Anchor Inn Christmas
Race to the Beach

SEABREEZE WEDDING CHAPEL:

The Bride's Dream Wedding

The Bride's Pink Shoes

The Bride's Christmas Dress

The Runaway Bride's Vow

The Bride's Antique Ring

WHISTLE STOP ROMANCE SERIES:

A Moment to Love

A Moment to Dance

A Moment on the Lips

A Moment to Cherish

A Moment at Christmas

TANGLED CHARMS:

Sprinkled with Love

A Mistletoe Kiss

GREEK PARADISE ESCAPE:

Greek Heir to Claim Her Heart

It Started with a Royal Kiss

Second Chance with the Bridesmaid

WEDDING BELLS IN LAKE COMO:

Bound by a Ring & a Secret

Falling for Her Convenient Groom

ONCE UPON A FAIRYTALE:

Beauty & Her Boss

Miss White & the Seventh Heir

Fairytale Christmas with the Millionaire

THE BARTOLINI LEGACY:

The Prince and the Wedding Planner

The CEO, the Puppy & Me

The Italian's Unexpected Heir

GREEK ISLAND BRIDES:

Carrying the Greek Tycoon's Baby

Claiming the Drakos Heir

Wearing the Greek Millionaire's Ring

Click here to find all of Jennifer's titles and buy links.

Made in United States
Troutdale, OR
11/16/2025

41995275R00149